Little Mysteries

Little Mysteries

Tonya K. Smith

MODELBENDERS PRESS

*In Loving Memory of
Daddy, Rebecca and Cheri*

Table of Contents

CHAPTER 1

The Viewing Public

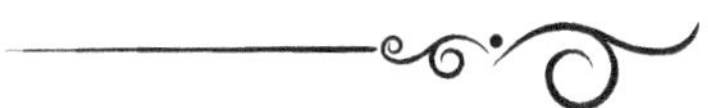

Most people don't believe there is any mystery in their lives. They go about their days working, raising families, and vacationing without much thought about the people around them. Of course, they are deeply involved with their own families and a few close friends, but rarely do people really open their eyes to see that there are people around them who are mysteries waiting to be solved. The interesting point is that rarely do they have to look further than the street on which they live to find a puzzling person; someone who has a cloudy past; someone who can't be explained.

This was the case in the neighborhood where I grew up. Our neighbors had some commonalities, but a few were just a little bit strange. At least that's what I thought. It didn't help that I was cursed with what my Mama and

Daddy called "a vivid imagination resulting in hyperbole". It took me a while to figure out they were calling me a liar, but I simply saw it as telling the truth as I saw it. So when I saw something of interest I tended to spice up the explanation a bit. I considered myself to be the Mark Twain of 70th street. I loved telling stories based on fact, so this is what this story is. It is up to you to figure out how to separate the truth from what I have embellished.

I think most people present themselves to the viewing public as "based on fact", but it isn't really who they are. Who they really are shows up when they think no one is looking. Just ask any politician, preacher, or any other public official and they will tell you the same.

For example, in our old neighborhood there was a lady who hung herself in her garage. It's true. The funny thing is that no one knew why. Of course you are thinking there's nothing strange about suicide it happens every day. This is unfortunately true, but what you don't know is that this lady was the one who inspired me to begin observing people and finding little mysteries within my own life. I credit her for inspiring me to find out her story and the circumstances surrounding her death.

The Suicide House

It was Halloween night 1973. I was eight years old and my older sister Vickie was ten. We were trick or treating with our friends Bobby, Tonda, Cheri, Tina, Demona, and Darren. These were our neighbors and we played together every day for years. Vickie was the oldest and therefore our leader. We had left my younger sister Rebecca at home because she was three and would be too scared to go out at night. Also, Mama had to pass out candy to the other trick or treaters. We came to the little brown corner house that was at the opposite corner from where my house was. Suddenly, Vickie stopped and said,

"Let's skip this house."

"Why?" I asked.

"The lady that lived there hung herself in the garage, and Mama told me not to take y'all there."

Unlike me, Vickie was purportedly brutally honest so no one questioned her and we moved on to the next house. As for me though, something about that incident just wouldn't let me go. I think it was perhaps because of the tone in Vickie's voice. Vickie wasn't afraid of anything or anybody, so the fact that the lady had hung herself must have been true because there was fear in Vickie's voice. Later that night in our room after we had binged on candy, I asked her about what she had said.

"Mama told me not to take y'all there; when I asked why she told me about the lady."

This was too much. I have to say that my Mama's knowledge of such an event elevated her already lofty position in my eyes. However, the fact that Mama knew that the lady hung herself was not enough to keep her from letting us go to that house so I decided to ask her about it the next day.

The next day at school, Mrs. Reed, my teacher, scolded us for being too tired to do our multiplication. Mrs. Reed was an older lady who had taught Moses the Egyptian alphabet, and her attitude towards children and teaching hadn't changed in all that time. The fact was that Mrs. Reed didn't like me. I always made good grades in her class, and finished assignments before time was called, so I always had a book ready to help pass the time. For some reason, this irked Mrs. Reed. When she caught me reading after an assignment she would say,

"Tonya, put that book away this instant it isn't reading time!"

I found it peculiar that Mrs. Reed's name seemed to be in opposition to what she wanted me to do in my spare time. She was also obsessed with her little timer that she used for every assignment. I think she aspired to be an Olympic timekeeper, because everything we did was timed. I mean everything, from going to the bathroom, walking anywhere in school, playing on the playground and even sharpening our pencils.

One time a boy I liked named Sean sharpened his pencil for more than the ten seconds allowed. Mrs. Reed broke the end off and told him to sharpen it again in the time allotted. Sean looked at her like she had grown a new head, and sharpened that pencil so fast he almost threw his shoulder out. He looked at her with satisfaction, sat down and proceeded to draw the most obscene picture of Mrs. Reed. She had boogers coming out of her nose, a loud burp in a balloon coming from her mouth and a fart coming from her rear end. Since I sat next to Sean, I saw it first and tried to keep it quiet while I was laughing my head off. Me and Sean's friendship was solidified when the picture was taken up and I said I had drawn it. Since I was a "good girl" all Dr. Overby, our principal said was that I should restrict my free time to something constructive like reading. Now I had the principal's special instructions to read in my free time. Funny how things work out sometimes.

Mrs. Reed had scolded us because we complained about being too tired to do our multiplication.

"No doubt, your parents let you run around your neighborhoods until heaven knows what hour so you could harass your neighbors into giving you candy. It is shameful your parents let you celebrate a heathen holiday like Halloween."

I didn't know what heathen meant but I know my parents weren't bad, so I raised my hand.

"Yes, Tonya?"

"Mrs. Reed, what is a heathen?"

"Good Lord Child, it is someone who doesn't believe in the Good Lord."

"Mrs. Reed, Mama and Daddy believe in God, but they let me go trick or treating so I was just wondering."

Really I was trying to clear Mama and Daddy from the heathen status in front of my classmates because I didn't want them to think I was a heathen too.

"Are you trying to be smart with me?"

"No ma'am I was just asking."

Mrs. Reed eyeballed me suspiciously, but let the matter drop. We began our multiplication papers and when I was finished I took out the copy of "Charlotte's Web" my Uncle had given me for my birthday. I was on my second of seven readings of the book and was just about to come to the part where Charlotte dies.

"Tonya, are you finished with your mathematics?" Mrs. Reed asked.

"Yes. Do I need to turn it in or are we going to check it ourselves?"

"We will check it ourselves when the timer buzzes, so please check your answers."

"I already did Mrs. Reed, and I think I got them all right.

"Well, bring your paper here so I can see for myself."

I took my paper to her desk and she asked me to wait while she checked my paper. This was a scenario that had taken place since the beginning of the school year. I got things finished and Mrs. Reed would check them, then she would give me extra work, I would finish that, and then I would read again. This irked Mrs. Reed time and time again, because I always finished first, and always wanted to read. After a couple of minutes Mrs. Reed told me to complete the next page in our workbook and then check the answers. I did this before the buzzer rang and pulled out "Charlotte's Web".

"Tonya, did you finish that other page?"

"Yes Maam."

"Land sakes child then do the next one. I cannot understand why you don't have more initiative."

I didn't know what Mrs. Reed was talking about, but sometimes it was just better to let things go. I did the next page and just when I finished the buzzer rang. Mrs. Reed told us to exchange papers with our neighbor so we could check our answers. Sean raised his hand and asked,

"Mrs. Reed, Tonya's paper is already checked so what do I do?"

"Sit quietly and wait until we are finished."

Mrs. Reed began calling out the answers and I checked Sean's paper. Sean wasn't very good at math so he got some of the problems wrong. It soon became apparent that Sean was going to get a bad grade on this assignment so I stopped marking answers wrong. I thought I was doing him a favor because sometimes he cried when he got a bad grade and then people would make fun of him. As secretly as I knew how, I erased Sean's answers and put in the correct ones. Sean saw what I was doing and kept still and quiet too. Finally, Mrs. Reed told us to put the score at the top of the page and then to pass them in. I thought I was home free until stupid Darla, the biggest goody goody you ever saw piped in.

"Mrs. Reed?" called Darla.

"Yes, Dear?" Mrs. Reed crooned. She just loved Darla.

"Were we supposed to fill in the right answer if the person got it wrong?"

"No, Darla, why do you ask?"

"Well, I saw Tonya doing that with Sean's paper so I did it on Sherry's too."

"I see." Mrs. Reed was glaring at me.

"Let's just pass in the papers and I will rescore each one correctly. Tonya I would like to speak to you and Sean while the rest of the class is at recess. Class, you have two minutes on the timer to get ready for recess."

Most of the class was already to go, but some of the girls like stupid Darla had to change their shoes from their good school shoes to their outside playing shoes.

Most of us only got one pair of shoes to wear to school, because we walked to school. Darla rode with her Mama every day and kissed her goodbye in front of the school. When everyone was ready, Mrs. Reed dismissed them for recess. Sean and I stayed behind in our desks. My friend Janet patted my shoulder on her way out as an encouragement.

"Tonya, would you like to explain yourself?" Mrs. Reed began.

"Well, I thought it might help Sean to have the right answers so he could see what he did wrong." I lied.

"Now, Tonya isn't it my job to be the teacher?"

"Yes Ma'am."

"I think you were trying to help your friend not get a bad grade isn't that right?" She saw right through me.

"Yes Ma'am. I'm sorry" I lied again. I wasn't sorry at all.

"Now Sean, did you know Tonya was doing this?"

"Not until I saw her mark the second or third one." I loved Sean for his honesty and his dreamy brown eyes.

"When you saw her doing that why didn't you say anything to me?" Mrs. Reed was such an Inquisitor sometimes.

"Well, I didn't want her to get in trouble, and if I get bad grades Mama and Daddy get really mad."

Sean was hoping to prey on her guilty conscience. Too bad Mrs. Reed didn't have one.

"Well, I am going to call both your parents and discuss the matter with them. Then we will decide what your punishment will be."

I knew I was dead meat. Mama had always taught us to follow the rules, because the rules had been put in place by people who knew what was necessary to run things smoothly. She had also told us that if we got in trouble at school, then there would be more waiting for us at home. I was certain Sean's Mama had said the same because those beautiful brown eyes began to leak. Mrs. Reed looked at the two of us and sent us out to recess. I knew we only had a short time outside, but I wanted to get away from Mrs. Reed. Sean sort of dragged behind me, but when we got to the door I gave him a quick smile and joined Janet and a few other girls jumping rope. Sean's face brightened and he went to play kickball with the boys who were one player short.

Later that afternoon when all of us were walking home from school, Vickie asked me about what had happened. Apparently, the scandal had reached the fifth grade and since I was Vickie's little sister, she wanted to know if her reputation had been besmirched. I told Vickie what happened, and she just laughed and began to taunt me with the regular rhyme of budding love.

"Tonya and Sean sittin in a tree,

K-I-S-S-I-N-G,

First comes love,

Then comes marriage,

Then comes Tonya with a baby carriage."

"You're stupid!" I yelled with embarrassment.

"At least I'm not in looooove." Vickie crooned.

We had just turned the corner to go down the street to our house. Vickie continued to taunt me until we were just about to come to the "suicide house". This is what we called the house where the lady hung herself. Vickie told us to stop and cross over to the other side of the street, so me and Tonda, and Tina, Cheri, Bobby and Demona did just that silently while looking out of the corners of our eyes at the house. When we got passed, we crossed the street again and continued our way home.

Apparently, the mothers in the neighborhood had sort of an agreement that was something like this. The children would come home from school, finish homework, then go outside and play until six o'clock dinner and then could go outside again if they didn't have chores to do. This arrangement had been put in place and had been followed for as long as any of us were in school. Vickie and I went inside and went straight to the kitchen where Mama had a snack for us and something to drink.

Mama had taken a part time job at the local newspaper in the complaints department so she could still be at home when Vickie and I got home from school. Little Rebecca went to a church's preschool near downtown where Mama worked so she went with Mama in the mornings and came back at about 1:00 pm. Mama was tired sometimes mostly she said from listening to people complain about their newspaper being delivered incorrectly or not at all. Sometimes it made her grumpy talking about those complaints, but sometimes she would giggle about how upset people got about their paper being delivered in their flower beds instead of their driveways. Today she seemed relatively cheerful, so I decided to finish my snack and then ask about the lady down the street.

After my Oreos and milk, I put my glass in the sink next to Mama who was rinsing out the morning dishes. I wasn't happy about seeing the morning dishes, because it was my turn to wash tonight after supper and there would be extra for me to do. I thought for a moment about how to ask about the lady. I decided the direct approach was best.

"Mama, why did that lady hang herself in her garage?"

Mama almost dropped a plate.

"Well, honey let me put it this way. The lady down the street, Mrs. Kemp was her name, was very sad. She was sad because she was unhappy and she couldn't make her husband happy."

I was glad Mama was straight with me, but she still managed to keep her dignity in a touchy situation.

"But Mama, why did she hang herself?"

"Well, she was so unhappy that she killed herself."

Mama had told me the truth, without going into details, so I was satisfied for the moment. Then Mama had a question for me.

"By the way, Tonya, Mrs. Reed called me at work today to tell me something about you helping a boy cheat at school. Do you want to tell me about it?"

"Mama, I wasn't trying to help Sean cheat. I changed some of his wrong answers to right ones on his paper because he cries if he gets a bad grade." I decided to be honest with Mama.

"Also, because she loves him!" Vickie chimed in.

"That's enough Vickie, this isn't your concern."

"Well, Tonya you know you probably would have helped Sean more if instead of changing his answer, just writing the correct answer next to his so he could see the correct answer and figure out for himself what he did wrong."

"Okay Mama, I'll do that instead next time." I was hoping the whole punishment phase might pass.

"Now wait a minute. I don't think you understand. You still did something wrong so there will be consequences. I think that for the rest of the week you will be doing all our dishwashing. That way you will have plenty of time to think about a better way to help Sean with his math other than just cheating for him. At the end of the week, I think you should have come up with at least three different ways to help Sean, and I want you to tell me what they are on Friday."

"Okay Mama. Do I have to do my other chores too?"

"Of course. That is what it means to be punished. You have to give up something like play time to pay for your wrongs."

"Okay Mama."

For the rest of the week, when I was doing dishes, I thought about how to help Sean a lot. I also thought of how grateful Sean would be and how those dreamy brown eyes would look at me when he saw how helpful I was. I was only annoyed a little that every time I washed dishes, Vickie dried them and would tease me if she caught me daydreaming. The rest of the week at school went by uneventfully and finally it was Friday.

Typically on Friday nights my friend Cheri's parents, Kaye and Jerry came over to play forty-two with my parents. This weekly domino game had started a few years back, so each week my friend Cheri and I would play with her vast collection of Barbies, and all the accessories including the Camper or Plane, and Car, while our parents played and talked about whatever was going on in the world or in our neighborhood. Mostly Kaye worried about her oldest son and how it was getting close to his 18th birthday. Everyone knew that when a boy turned 18, they had to register for the Selective Service for the Vietnam War. Also, Jerry would talk about business and sometimes our parents would make vacation plans for our two families to go camping together.

I often wondered if they realized that Cheri and I listened to every word. I was always listening for two reasons; gossip and cursing. Cheri's Mama cursed every once in a while which always made me giggle. I giggled because my Mama would blush and kind of make a silent "Oh" every time. One time Kaye knocked over her sweet tea and spilled it all over the card table, Cheri's Daddy, and all the dominoes. She "damned" so many times in a row in rapid succession that Mama and Daddy and Jerry all burst out laughing. Kaye apologized profusely to me and Cheri and that only made us laugh harder.

Anyway, Cheri's parents and Mama and Daddy were playing when Kaye asked what Mama knew about Mrs. Kemp. Mama knew that she was being pumped for information to pass along to the rest of the neighborhood. She pretended not to hear the question.

"What?" Mama gave a warning nod in me and Cheri's direction.

"Now Dolores," began Kaye,"You work down there at that newspaper, and I know you must have heard something from those reporters down there."

Mama repeated almost verbatim what she had told me in the kitchen the previous Monday.

"Well, I heard that Mr. Kemp used to beat her and she just couldn't take it anymore," Kaye retorted.

I couldn't believe what I was hearing. My Mama had always said that men who did that weren't good Christians and that God would judge them. I never thought we would have a wife beater living on our street. Cheri's face must have shown the same shock because Mama said,

"Little pitchers have big ears."

Of course this was my and Cheri's cue to pretend we hadn't heard so that the adults would continue gossiping. Kaye answered,

"Well, you never know what happens behind closed doors, but Mrs. Weld said she had seen bruises on that woman's face before."

Mama replied,

"It's just plain sad. I hope things settle down now."

I didn't know what Mama meant by that, but I thought it would be best if Cheri and I played somewhere else. We went to my bedroom to talk about what we'd heard with Vickie who was listening to the radio. We repeated the story and Vickie listened the sort of dismissed us by saying we shouldn't be so nosy. I hated it when she acted all big and cool. After all she was only two years older than me, but I guess you know more when you're in fifth grade.

Thanksgiving

After a few weeks of walking past the suicide house on the way to and from school, my thoughts turned toward Thanksgiving and Christmas. I loved Thanksgiving. We would all go over to my Grandma and Grandpa's house for Thanksgiving dinner. My Grandma was a wonderful cook and she had a recipe for cornbread dressing that was so delicious. All of us have tried to duplicate her recipe, but I can honestly say I have only gotten close a couple of times.

Grandma cooked all day to prepare a traditional feast of turkey, dressing, mashed potatoes, rolls, cranberry sauce and gravy. However, Grandma liked to throw in a couple of unusual items as well. Her favorite was pickled beets. I remember vividly how she would drain the juice out of the jar and put it in the refrigerator to chill. Later, she would take the little glass out and drink that juice. She would smile and say,

"I just love this juice. It makes me feel all happy."

Then she would follow that with a couple of quick drinks of vanilla extract so her breath would smell good. I don't think Grandma realized that she was drinking about 90 proof alcohols and therefore the equivalent of a couple of shots of Jack Daniels. She would have been mortified, because Grandma was one of the most devout Christians I ever knew. Grandpa didn't seem to mind her little indiscretions either because Grandma became quite agreeable after her little treat.

Grandma also made candied sweet potatoes, which was made especially for my Daddy. Daddy was the only one who liked them, but Grandma just loved Daddy so she made them for him. I think she especially liked Daddy, because he was always willing to help her out with things. For example, one time she asked Daddy to make her a clothesline for the backyard. She wanted it made of metal poles with metal wiring to go across, because that way the clothes wouldn't sag. Daddy welded her two posts and strung the wire which made Grandma happy. Neither one thought about what would happen when a thunderstorm came through, but Grandma seemed fascinated by her free fireworks display every time it rained.

In addition to Grandma's cooking, Mama always made the pies that would be dessert. She made pumpkin, pecan and some weird pie called minced meat pie. I loved

Mama's pecan pie, but wondered who in their right mind would eat a pie full of minced meat. My Uncle's wife, Aunt Linda, was into cooking high classed foods called cuisine. That meant that whatever she brought looked and smelled weird especially her green bean casserole. It was green and kinda soupy with little bits of red stuff that just made it look disgusting. Vickie used to say that Aunt Linda made it out of the ground up witches she had caught on Halloween night. Aunt Linda would enter Grandma's house with a sort of flourish and exclaim,

"Here is the specialty of the house!"

Sometimes I would catch Mama rolling her eyes before taking the casserole to the kitchen.

Once everyone had arrived and hugged and kissed and all that we would sit down to eat. All the adults would sit in Grandma's tiny dining area and we kids would sit in the living room. Including Vickie, Rebecca and I was Marla and Gary my Aunt Linda's kids and Nicholas and eventually Christopher my Uncle Randy's kids. My Uncle Randy was kind of the rebel of Mama and Uncle Gerald's family, but I thought he was neat. He wore really long hair and his wife was beautiful I thought, because she always had on lots of eyeliner. My cousin Marla was the princess of her family and boy did it ever show. She was pretty but spoiled and kind of rotten. Her favorite thing to do was to brag about her latest accomplishments. Aunt Linda would encourage her and say how smart she was. I just thought she was ridiculous.

After we had stuffed our faces, my favorite part of Thanksgiving came. Grandpa would gather all us kids around him and would tell us a story. Grandpa was a great storyteller. He was very animated and made all sorts of animal noises. Once he made the sound of a bear so convincingly, Rebecca started crying and ran to Mama. After Grandpa told his story he told us that it was our turn. The kid who told the best story would get a nickel. I always went last and I borrowed the best parts from the others' stories. Grandpa liked that so I won the nickel lots of times, but whenever I did Marla would start fussing until her Mama would say something like,

"Stop fussing, I'll give you a nickel when we get home."

Mama always seemed to need to excuse herself to the kitchen when this happened. After a while, it was time for dessert. Mama would slice the pies, but it was Aunt Linda who served the pie to all the men first. She would smile her phony smile and serve the pies as if she made them herself. Mama was too polite to tell Aunt Linda to shut up and sit down, but she wasn't so shy as to ask Linda if she wanted to take home the leftover casserole since hardly anyone ate it. This was the way Thanksgiving went for years.

CHAPTER 4

Christmas Party

As much as I loved Thanksgiving, Christmas was the best. Christmas meant decorating, baking, shopping, and of course visiting Santa and Santa Land. It was also the time when my parents hosted the annual young couples class Christmas party at our house. The young couples class was the class that Mama and Daddy went to on Sunday mornings at church. It was made up of people their ages which meant most of them had children me and Vickie's ages. Typically between thirty and forty people crowded into our tiny house, and if the weather wasn't too cold, us kids would play out in the front yard under the glow of the streetlight. Our parents would stay inside and play games or do whatever it is adults do at a party.

For days before the party Mama cleaned and baked and fretted over every detail. She loved having people over, but she always worried that she didn't have enough food. Of course, she didn't need to worry because everyone brought things to share. The night of the party, people began arriving so it was my job to take the ladies' coats and purses and put them on Mama and Daddy's bed. Vickie was supposed to help Mama in the kitchen and Rebecca was to just look cute which she always did very well because of her curly hair and huge blue eyes.

As the party progressed kids my age, who were my church friends, showed up too. Sometimes we played board games, but this particular year Vickie and I had something special planned. We decided to wait until the adults were too busy to notice us and then we were going to take some of the brave kids down to the "suicide house". We waited and finally told the story to the older kids and asked who wanted to go. Several wanted to so we began walking down the street towards the house. As we walked we all admired the Christmas lights our neighbors had put up. We stopped briefly at one of our neighbors the Crawford's, who had a lit up nativity scene. My friend Jill asked,

"How come baby Jesus isn't lit up yet?"

"They only light him up on Christmas Eve."

"Why?"

"Well, they are Catholic and that is part of their tradition at Christmas."

Mama had explained this to me last year so I was proud to show off all my knowledge of the Catholic faith. Jill wasn't satisfied.

"So Jesus the Son of God only gets one night lit up and everything else including the camel gets how many days?"

"Well, they usually light everything else the day after Thanksgiving."

"Weird, I think it should be the other way around."

"But that's not the rules." I said rather dismally at not having the whole story.

By this time we had reached the "suicide house" and had crossed the street to get a better look at it. There were no Christmas lights on the house. I told everyone that maybe it was because when the lady hung herself it cut off all the electricity and the lights wouldn't work.

"No, stupid. If that was true then the porch light wouldn't work either," Vickie pointed out.

"Do you think the lady went to hell?" Jill kind of half whispered.

I had never heard Jill curse before and I was shocked. Jill saw the surprise on everyone's face and explained,

"My Daddy says that hell isn't a bad word, because it is in the Bible."

This made sense. Jill's Daddy was a deacon at our church and he would know better than anybody what words were curse words and what words weren't. After thinking a little Vickie said she didn't know if the lady went to hell or not and that we should vote on it. Vickie always wanted to vote on everything, because she wanted to be the President of the United States one day. We voted six votes to three that the lady went to hell. The three that voted that she didn't were too afraid to vote that she did. It must have been a loud vote because suddenly the front window light went on at the "suicide house". We ran as fast as we could back to our house.

The adults heard us and asked what we were doing. Vickie answered,

"Just playing."

This answer satisfied our mothers who were anxious to exchange recipes with each other. Since we seemed safe, we all began to play again. At some point we grew tired of playing freeze tag so Jill suggested we play "Suicide House". This was a reenactment of what we believed had happened to the lady. Also, it meant that the kids that had been too chicken to see the house could still get the thrill of being there.

Vickie played the lady, Bobby played the husband, I played the Devil, and the rest played my minions who dragged the lady to hell after she hung herself. We gathered up a few props like some rope we found in the garage, and a rake that served as my pitchfork. We had the audience of the chicken kids sit on the grass and the play began.

Vickie and Bobby came in. Bobby yelled at Vickie,

"I see you burned dinner again! Are you stupid?"

He then fake slapped Vickie who replied,

"You'll be sorry for that."

Bobby said,

"I'm going to sleep on the couch!"

Bobby began making snoring noises while Vickie sneaked by him, put the rope around her neck and hung herself. This was my cue. I entered and in my most maniacal voice shouted,

"Welcome to Hell!"

My minions picked up Vickie and brought her to me. I laughed and said

"People who kill themselves spend all eternity with me!"

I must have played the Devil really good because some of the kids in the audience began to cry. Just about then Mama called me and Vickie in to pass out the coats and purses. The guests began to leave and finally everyone was gone. It was the best Christmas party ever.

After all the guests left, it was time for me and Vickie to get ready for bed. We put on our pajamas and brushed our teeth. We got into bed and waited for Mama and Daddy to come in for our prayers. Finally, after Rebecca was in bed they came in. Vickie said her usual prayer, but I had something different on my mind. I began with the usual, thanking God for the day and all the family members and for Jesus, but I had been thinking about the lady down the street so I said,

"Dear God, please help the lady who hung herself not go to hell." I ended and opened my eyes. Mama had a shocked face and Daddy has his "you're gonna get a whipping face" on. Vickie had hidden under the covers. Daddy asked,

"Where did you hear that word?"

I explained about Jill's Daddy saying is wasn't a curse word and I caught Daddy smiling a little. Then he told me not to say that word again, and left Mama to have a chat with us girls. Mama sat down on Vickie's bed, and told me to come over. This was serious. We were never allowed to get out from under the covers after prayers. Mama told us never to say "hell" again and to never say anything to anybody about the lady down the street.

"Why, Mama?" I asked.

"It isn't our business."

"But Mama, Vickie and I walk by that house every day on the way to school and I think it is my business to know that there was someone who was beaten up by her husband and hung herself."

There aren't words to describe my Mama's look on her face. In fact, it changed so quickly from anger to shock to horror that they all became one. Mama said she was tired and we would talk more in the morning. I went back to my bed and Mama kissed me and Vickie and turned out the light on her way out.

"You are a new kind of stupid," Vickie whispered in the dark.

"What did I say?"

"Just shut up you dummy!"

I could hear urgent whispers coming from my parent's bedroom. I got out of bed and went to their doorway.

"Mama, I'm sorry." I said quietly.

"It's okay baby, now go back to bed."

"I love you Mama and Daddy."

"We love you too, now go back to bed."

For a long time my parents whispered. They whispered until I fell asleep.

CHAPTER 5

New Revelations

*W*hen I woke up the next day, I was ready for action. Saturdays meant three things; cartoons, playing and chores. Saturdays were Mama's cleaning days since she was working part time at the newspaper. She was working so we would have some extra money for Christmas presents. She worked at the newspaper during the day, but at night she worked for about four hours as a gift wrapper in a local department store. Mama was really busy, but she seemed to like being out of the house and earning some money.

I was the last one up that morning and when I went into the kitchen, Rebecca was already watching Bugs Bunny so Mama could clean the bathrooms. Vickie's job was to help Daddy outside and my job was to keep Rebecca occupied so Mama could clean. Even though Mama was a good mother and housekeeper, she absolutely hated cleaning. She was often vexed when it came to cleaning, so the best thing to do was to make yourself scarce, or you could be recruited to do some awful chore, like cleaning your room.

This particular Saturday, Mama was particularly sour because she still had cleaning up to do from the party. Daddy and Vickie were already outside so Rebecca and I were left to deal with Mama's bad mood. I don't know why I picked this particular morning to berate Mama with question about the lady, but I suppose the subject was like forbidden fruit.

While Rebecca ate her Cocoa Puffs, I went into the little bathroom where Mama was scrubbing. She was on her knees scrubbing the bottom of the bathtub. I should have waited, but I was impatient so I asked,

"Mama, why couldn't that lady make her husband happy?"

"What lady" Mama asked distractedly.

"The lady that hung herself."

"Oh for pity's sake, I don't know! Maybe she didn't clean the bathroom right." Mama snapped.

"That doesn't seem like a good reason to hang yourself," I just couldn't let it go.

"Out!" Mama cried and I knew I'd better skedaddle.

Why couldn't I get a straight answer? I went to check on Rebecca who had finished her breakfast and was trying to dress herself. She was halfway out of her Strawberry Shortcake nightgown but she couldn't get her arm out. We went into Rebecca's bedroom and I picked out her pants and shirt for the day. Mama had let me pick out Rebecca's clothes almost every day since she was born. After I got Rebecca dressed we went outside. Daddy and Vickie weren't doing any yard work because it was December, but some of the neighborhood kids were playing football in the street. Vickie was quarterback of course, and Daddy was messing around with the truck. I went over to Daddy and asked what he was doing.

"I'm measuring the truck so I can put another gas tank on it. I asked a guy down at the shop if he knew how to do it, and he said he would help me out.

"Why do we need another tank?"

"Well, when we go camping this summer, we won't have to stop for gas as often if we have two tanks. We can just switch from one tank to the other."

"Are we going with Cheri and them?"

"Yep. We're thinking of going someplace new this year even deeper in the mountains."

"Hey Daddy, I want to ask you something."

"Okay, what is it?"

"Does Mama make you happy?"

"Yes, I suppose so, why?"

"All the time?"

"Yes, all the time."

"Don't you ever get mad at her?"

"Sometimes, but even if I get mad she still makes me happy."

This was confusing. How can a person be mad and happy at the same time? Daddy noticed my silence and didn't say anything for a minute.

"Hand me that pencil in my glove box."

I handed him the pencil and watched his thick fingers grip it and mark a thick pencil line on the floorboard of the truck.

"What's that for?" I asked.

"That's where the switch is going to go that will switch the fuel lines from one tank to the other. Now why are you asking about me and your Mama's happiness?"

I had almost forgotten our previous line of conversation. It was funny with Daddy. No matter how I wanted to I couldn't hide my feelings or try to lie to him. I suppose it was that he trusted me, and that made me want to be truthful. Also, he was a hard disciplinarian when it came to lying. I looked at him and spelled it out.

"Daddy, Mama said that the lady down the street hung herself because she couldn't make her husband happy. So I was thinking that what if Mama didn't make you happy. Would you beat her up like Cheri's Mama said and then that would make Mama so upset that she would kill herself?

I thought Daddy was mad for a minute because of the look on his face. He stared and took a deep breath. He scratched his head and shifted in the seat of the truck. He chuckled a little.

"I swear sometime I can't believe how smart you are."

I didn't know what he meant but I smiled at the compliment.

"I guess you take after your Mama that way. Number one, sometimes I get mad at your Mama and sometimes she gets mad at me. Sometimes we yell at each other even, but we still love each other. I would never, ever, beat your Mama. Grown men that beat their wives are cowards. Number two, I think your Mama gets sad sometimes, but she gets over it. Number three, you shouldn't be listening to everything Cheri's Mama says because sometime she tends to make stories more interesting if you know what I mean."

"You mean, she's got a vivid imagination resulting in hyperbole just like me?"

Daddy started laughing so hard Rebecca stopped her Big Wheel and laughed too. When Daddy caught his breath he managed,

"I guess so, but don't tell her that it might make her mad. I will tell you a secret though if you promise not to tell your Mama."

"I promise, what, what, what?"

"Well, after Mrs. Kemp died, she's the lady you're referring to, your Mama and some of the other ladies went down there with food so when her family came for the funeral Mr. Kemp would have something to feed them. They were a little scared and nervous, because Mrs. Kemp had died there. Anyway, Mr. Kemp came to the door and your Mama gave him the food. Mr. Kemp invited them in so they could help him figure out where to put all the dishes they had brought. Your Mama said that there was a huge picture of Mrs. Kemp in the front room. It was life size. That means it was the same size as Mrs. Kemp. Your Mama said Mrs. Campbell sort of gasped when she saw it. Your Mama also said Mr. Kemp was really a nice guy and she couldn't understand why Mrs. Kemp was unhappy. After they left your Mama and Mrs. Campbell decided not to bother him again. I think that's a wise idea for you too."

When Daddy finished his story he got out of the truck and started around for the garage. Rebecca was trying to ride her Big Wheel as fast as Vickie was running for a touchdown. I got my bicycle out and rode to my friend's Cheri's house down the street. As soon as she let me in we went to her bedroom to play Barbies. I told her everything my Daddy had said. Her eyes got bigger and bigger. When I was done she said she had heard something new too.

Cheri said her mother had visited Mrs. White who had a beauty shop right where her garage used to be. Mrs. White lived about halfway between the corner I lived on and the corner of the suicide house. Mrs. White had her husband convert her garage to a three chair beauty shop because she needed the extra money, and she had her beautician's license. All the ladies on our block either had their hair done there or had their Sunday wigs styled there. Mama occasionally had me either run her wig over or pick it up. Once when I picked it up, I fell and got it a little dirty. Mama was mad because she didn't have enough money to have it done again, so she had to wear her own hair to church the next day.

Anyway, Cheri's Mama was having her hair dyed so she got to visiting with Mrs. White and Mrs. Crawford who was having her hair set. Of course, the conversation got around to Mrs. Kemp's demise. Mrs. Crawford used to play cards with Mrs. Kemp and some other ladies from the Catholic Church. Mrs. Crawford and Mrs. Kemp were the only Catholics on the block. Everybody else was Baptist, Southern Baptist, or Methodist. We were Church of Christ, and the family behind us and across the alley was Greek Orthodox. The family behind us and across the alley was not only Greek Orthodox, but they were actually from Greece. Every Easter they would roast a lamb in their backyard and they also had a pigeon coop.

Mrs. Crawford said that Mrs. Kemp and she had played their regular bridge game the day before Mrs. Kemp hung herself. She also told Mrs. Campbell and Mrs. White that Mrs. Kemp seemed fine and had actually won at cards. Mrs. Kemp left Mrs. Crawford's house went home and the next day hung herself. Mrs. Crawford said that when the police came to talk to her about Mrs. Kemp, she told them the truth and said that Mrs. Kemp seemed fine the day before. The police said they had to ask as a matter of procedure. After the police left, Mrs. Crawford went over to the Kemp's to tell Mr. Kemp what she had told the police. Mrs. Crawford said that when she got over to the Kemp's the front door was open and only the screen door was closed. She said she heard Mr. Kemp talking so she peeked through the screen and she realized Mr. Kemp was talking to that life sized portrait of Mrs. Kemp. She said it was so sad she began to cry and had to go home.

I was just bursting at the seams with curiosity now. Why would Mr. Kemp be talking to a painting? What did he say? Is he still doing it? Cheri and I spent the rest of the afternoon discussing these new developments. When Mama called me home it was time to get my hair rolled for church the next day.

As Mama set the curlers in my hair we didn't say much. I was busy thinking and Mama was holding the bobby pins in her mouth. Mama was very particular about how my hair looked for church. She made sure my curlers were straight and even so that my hair would dry by morning. I must have been particularly quiet because finally she put the comb down and said,

"What's on your mind?"

"Nothing."

"We what did you and Cheri do today?"

"Just played Barbies."

"Well it must have been exciting since you are so talkative about it."

I decided that maybe this would be a good time to ask Mama about the painting.

"Mama, please don't get mad, but I want to ask you something."

"Why would I get mad at a question?"

"Well, I guess it's because of what it is."

"Well I won't get mad as long as you keep still."

"Okay, you promised. I wanted to ask you why Mr. Kemp talks to that painting of Mrs. Kemp."

It seemed as though over the last few days I had shocked my parents more that my allotment. Mama sighed a little and said,

"Honey, I think it could be many reasons, but if I had to guess it is because he misses her. Maybe talking to that picture makes him feel a little better.

"Mama what do you think he says to her? Do you think he feels bad because he beat her up?"

"Honey, those are just rumors. Besides, I went over there after it happened and he seemed like such a good guy. I don't think he beat her up. Sometimes I think people just make up stories. How did you know about that painting anyway?"

"Daddy told me about it."

"I should have guessed. Your Daddy can't keep a secret. I suppose he told you about Mrs. Kemp's clothes?"

"No, what about them?"

"Well, Mrs. Kemp had some very nice clothes. She even had a fur coat."

"So what?"

"Well honey, Mrs. Kemp's clothes were all very expensive. She even had designer clothes from New York City. One time she gave me a coat she said she couldn't wear anymore. You know my white one I wear to church?"

"Yeah, it's so soft. I love to pet that coat."

"I know. Anyway she gave it to me because she saw that I didn't have a good coat. After she died…"

"Hung herself," I corrected.

"Oh honey, I wish you wouldn't dwell on that. After she died Mr. Kemp waited about two or three months to clean out her closet. Mrs. Campbell and I helped him because he was just so sad."

This was a new revelation. Mama had been in that house two times. Mama continued.

"We donated some of her things and Mr. Kemp sold some and the he gave some to the neighborhood ladies. He was so gracious and kind, but you could tell he was really sad. If you look around the neighborhood you'll see some of Mrs. Kemp's things walking around."

"That's so weird. It's like her ghost is still around."

"Now honey stop that. I don't want you to start your imagination going crazy and you start telling stories to all the neighborhood kids. Now go get Rebecca, I need to do her hair."

When I went to get Rebecca, she was watching "Wild Kingdom" with Daddy. I sat down next to him.

"Mama needs you Rebecca, she's in the bathroom."

Rebecca ran off happily because she knew she was going to have Mama's attention for about an hour.

"What's going on?" I asked Daddy.

"Same as usual. They are chasing water buffaloes with a helicopter, Jim is jumping out to wrestle it down, and

Marlon Perkins is narrating. I hope they pay that Jim guy a lot of money. I wouldn't jump out of a helicopter for nothing, would you?"

"No way!"

We continued watching until Jim had successfully tagged and transported a water buffalo to a new location and Mutual of Omaha's Wild Kingdom ended. Mama finished Rebecca's hair and began working on Vickie's. Vickie was mad because she thought she was old enough to do her own hair. Vickie had very long blonde hair that she was very proud of, so it was important to make it look nice for church.

Finally, we girls had our hair in curlers and were off to bed. Rebecca easily went to bed, but Vickie and I usually stalled as long as possible by brushing our teeth really slowly, needing drinks of water etc....until Mama finally lost her composure and yelled,

"GO TO BED!"

Once Vickie and I were in our room it was a race to see who got in bed first. The last one on the bed had to turn off the light. Since I was afraid of the dark, and afraid something would grab my leg from under the bed, I had adopted a sort of running leap to my bed. If I was lucky, which wasn't often, I would land and Vickie would turn out the light. Then we would whisper back and forth until Mama and Daddy went to their room which was next to ours.

That night I whispered everything I knew about Mr. and Mrs. Kemp, her clothes and the painting. Vickie listened for a while and finally said,

"You know, you are not supposed to talk about dead people, especially those that kill themselves."

"Why not?"

"Because, everyone knows that someone who kill themselves was an unhappy soul."

"What do you mean?"

"Well, an unhappy person has an unhappy soul. Unhappy souls want to leave the unhappy person, so it makes them kill themselves so the soul is free to look around for somebody new to go in to."

"You mean Mrs. Kemp's soul is wandering around looking for a new body?"

"Yeah, especially someone who is happy a lot. That's why when I walk past that house I always try to look sad. That way Mrs. Kemp's soul won't try to get in me."

"You're lying!" I began to sing a song I had heard from my friend Jill.

> *"Revelation, Revelation,*
> *Four twenty-eight, four twenty-eight,*
> *Liars go to hell, liars go to hell,*
> *Burn sinner burn, burn sinner burn."*

"Mama, Tonya's cussing me out!"

Moments passed but Mama didn't come so Vickie said,

"If you don't shut up I'm going in there and telling Mama and then you'll be in for it."

I turned over and faced the window. Vickie finally went to sleep but I was busy thinking about what she said.

I figured she was lying, but just as I drifted off, I thought about the coat Mama had gotten from Mrs. Kemp.

Since it is common knowledge that the last thing a person thinks about colors their dreams, it is no surprise that I had a nightmare. I dreamed that it was the middle of the night and the doorbell rang. Strangely sweet, Mama said,

"I wonder who that could be?"

Even stranger was that Mama was wearing the coat Mrs. Kemp gave her. Mama opened the front door and it was Mrs. Kemp's soul. She said,

"I won't be happy till I have my coat back!"

Then Mama and Mrs. Kemp's soul began to kind of wrestle until Mama had the coat off. Mrs. Kemp's soul put it on and said,

" Just one more thing!"

Then Mrs. Kemp's soul stepped into Mama's body. Mama turned to me and said in Mrs. Kemp's voice,

"Now you'll have two mommies, one bad and one good, one bad and one good one bad and one good..."

I jerked awake because Vickie was punching my arm.

"Shut up, stupid!"

She was always so kind. I didn't dare tell her about my dream because she would just make fun of me. I turned over again and looked at the moon that peeked through the crack in the curtains on my window. When I fell asleep again thankfully Mrs. Kemp's soul let me rest in peace.

Prayer Requests

The next morning was Sunday which meant getting ready for Bible class and church. I put on clean panties, my Sunday dress, socks and shoes and went to the kitchen. Vickie was already there eating Cocoa Puffs. Rebecca was eating Pop Tarts and Mama was putting together the chicken and rice we would eat for dinner. This was my favorite dish so I always watched Mama make it from the bar that looked into the kitchen.

"Don't you want to eat something before I do your hair?"

"She's probably still scared," crooned Vickie from the table.

"Scared from what?" Mama asked distractedly as she cut up the chicken.

"Nothing Mama, just a bad dream I had last night."

"Oh, do you want to tell me about it?"

"No, I think I'll just watch you."

Mama smiled a little. She had just taken out the packet of innards that came inside the body cavity of the chicken. She carefully opened it to take out the liver. She was about to throw the rest out.

"What are the rest of those and how come you don't cook and eat them too?" I asked.

"Well, the liver is good for you, but this is the gizzard. I don't think it tastes very good. This is the neck, which I sometime use for chicken broth, but I like to boil it. "

The next thing Mama said just about knocked me off the barstool.

"And this is the heart. I don't like to eat the heart, because it's like eating the soul of the chicken."

Vickie almost choked on Cocoa Puffs. I knew she was thinking about Mrs. Kemp's soul too. Luckily Daddy started laughing his crazy, choking, crackly laugh because of something Alley Oop had said in the funny papers. I didn't ask any more questions, but simply watched Mama finish making the chicken and rice. Finally, she washed and dried her hands and said to go in her bedroom so she could do my hair.

When my hair was done, Mama finished dressing, and Daddy helped me, Vickie and Rebecca find our Bibles and coats and went out to start the car warming up. Mama was always the last one in the car. When Mama came out of the house, Vickie frogged me in the leg. Mama was wearing "the coat". She got in and as we passed the Kemp house,

Mr. Kemp was getting his Sunday paper. He looked up just in time to see Mama wave her usual friendly wave. Mr. Kemp smiled broadly and waved but as we passed I turned around and watched for a second. Mr. Kemp let his arm come down real slowly.

"Maybe he though he saw a ghost," whispered Vickie.

"Shut up!" I said a little too loudly.

"What's going on back there?" said Daddy.

Daddy took driving seriously so we were not to fight, or fuss in the car.

"Nothing Daddy" said Vickie sweetly.

Mama started talking to Daddy about different things happening and Daddy listened but didn't say too much. Where we got to church, Rebecca went to the three year old class, Vickie went to the fifth grade class, and I went to the third grade class. Mama and Daddy went to their young couples class.

When I got to class, my friend Jill had saved me a seat. My class was taught by two men who were brothers, Mr. Roy Thomas and Mr. Al Thomas. Mr. Roy and Mr. Al were slightly older than my parents, but Mr. Roy had a daughter who was a year younger than me. Mama and Daddy were friends with both Thomas families so I had to be good in class.

Whenever we started class they always asked who we needed to pray for. Usually I didn't make any input, but this particular morning I was thinking of Mr. Kemp. I raised my hand and Mr. Roy said,

"Good, Tonya. Who is it we need to pray for?"

"Mr. Kemp, my neighbor."

"Why do we need to pray for him?" I hadn't expected this question.

"Um, because he's sad."

"Why is he sad?"

I decided at that moment never to request prayers for somebody out loud ever again. If I'd known I was going to get the third degree I wouldn't have opened my fat mouth. Suddenly from beside me my friend Jill piped up.

"He is sad because he used to beat up Mrs. Kemp, and one day she got tired of it, went into her garage and hung herself."

Dead silence. Mr. Roy was stunned. I was stunned. The whole class was stunned. Jill added,

"That's what Tonya told me at the Christmas party Friday night."

She must have sensed the uneasiness in the room because the smile faded from her face. I knew I was dead meat when I got home from church.

Mr. Roy kind of sputtered out "Who else do we need to pray for?" hoping to distract the class from the previous statement. Of course the damage was done and another kid named Joe added,

"That's right Mr. Thomas. I was there too and so we voted and we voted 6 to 3 that the lady went to hell because she killed herself and that's a sin."

Mr. Roy sighed, took a deep breath and kind of aside said to Mr. Al, "It looks like we're not going to get to First Timothy this morning."

Mr. Al nodded and said," Maybe we should talk about sin a little this morning."

No one groaned out loud but we all knew what that meant. Sin was Mr. Al's favorite topic and he could spot a sin a mile away.

He began, "So is it true the lady hung herself?"

"Yes," I answered.

"Is it true that Mr. Kemp beat her?"

"Well, that what my other neighbor said."

"Did you ever see him beat her?"

"No," I answered figuring out that Mr. Al was pointing out the sin on me.

"Isn't spreading a story about someone that your aren't sure is true kind of like a lie? Isn't lying a sin?" he continued.

My friend Jill's song came to mind.

"Yes sir."

"Alright, that's sin number one. Now isn't God the ultimate judge of sinners?"

"Yes sir." I answered.

"Now you said you voted that the lady went to hell so isn't that taking God's place as judge?"

"Yes sir." I answered feeling a little better knowing that Vickie had sinned too.

"That's sin number two. Isn't bearing false witness against your neighbor a sin?"

"Yes sir," I had been through this drill before and I knew the only correct answer was "yes sir".

"That's sin number three. Now if God played by the rules of baseball you'd be out, but fortunately he had mercy and grace to cover us."

This was the part where we were all supposed to say amen, but I think we all knew that the less we said the better. I was already sweating and knew I was in for it when I got home.

"All right, I think we ought to think about what we're saying before we say it."

"Yes sir."

"I think that about cover the most important aspect of this situation, but is there anyone else we need to pray for?"

"How about the missionaries in Africa?" asked goody goody Angela.

Angela's Daddy was a doctor and she went to private Christian school. She always seemed to know the right thing to say and I was jealous of her for that. It's funny how people's names point out their personalities sometimes.

Mr. Roy and Mr. Al both approved of this request. After a minute or two we prayed for those missionaries, but in my head I prayed for Mr. Kemp too. Then I felt guilty because I thought maybe I was sinning going against my elders. We managed to get about the first three verses of First Timothy done when the bell rang for Bible class to be over. I hurried out of the room and went to Rebecca's class to pick her up. Her class was on the second floor with mine so I picked her up and then we met Mama and Daddy for services. Rebecca showed me her picture of Jesus she had colored in class. She was so proud that I overlooked the fact that Jesus was entirely purple. If nothing else, Rebecca was thorough.

"Look, no white parts," she beamed.

"Good!" I praised her.

The picture looked like Rebecca had melted the crayon so that it was a smooth shiny coat of purple. The little lambs at the bottom were also purple.

"You could make a purple sweater out of their wool," I commented. Rebecca smiled.

After Rebecca and I got to the foyer of the auditorium we met Mama, Daddy, Vickie, Grandma, and Grandpa. I loved sitting with Grandma and Grandpa because Grandpa sang tenor really well and really loud and Grandma always had Juicy Fruit gum in her purse. Mama didn't like us chewing gum but Grandma sneaked it to us anyway.

We went inside and sat down about a third of the way from the front. Services began with about six songs, then the communion. I was mystified by communion because I thought it was strange that in the first plate that came around, there was a huge cracker. However, all the adults had some sort of weird competition to see who could break off the smallest bit. I think my Grandma won a lot because sometimes she would suck the tiny pieces from between her fingers. The next thing to be passed was the grape juice. I know it was grape juice because one time Vickie dared me to take one. I did and drank it while Mama wasn't looking. The little cups were always filled only half way and I thought the men who passed the trays were stingy because they watched everybody drink their one tiny sip.

Last was the collection. This was my favorite part. I loved seeing all that money in the plate. Also, Mama had just begun giving me a nickel to put in myself. She gave Vickie a dime because she was older, but poor little Rebecca only got a penny to put in. I watched Grandma put in her check for five dollars, and tried to imagine what I would do with five dollars. I decided that I would buy more grape juice so that everybody could have a whole glass instead of those tiny cups the stingy servers gave out. I might even buy enough crackers for everyone too.

Once communion was over, our preacher Mr. Roberts got up to deliver the sermon. I was scared to death of Mr. Roberts because sometimes he yelled at us for no reason. But as scared of him as I was, I couldn't imagine being one of his children. Mr. Roberts had two sons he made sit right on the front pew. Sometimes if they go to fooling around Mr. Roberts would stop preaching just long enough to say something like "We're going to have a talk when we get home."

He wouldn't miss a beat so secretly I hoped the boys would be bad so I could hear Mr. Roberts call them out from the pulpit. Later, I dated one of those boys and he told me that often they got another sermon at home and they would actually beg for a spanking instead. But that is a different story.

This particular morning Mr. Roberts was preaching about Lazarus being raised from the dead by Jesus. I was kind of listening, but I had heard this story a hundred times in my short life, so I was busy looking for gum in Grandma's purse. I notice that Vickie was drawing on the back of one of the attendance cards, but I didn't pay attention until she passed it behind Grandma's head. This is what she drew: Jesus called Mrs. Kemp out of the tomb. Mrs. Kemp is chasing Mama yelling "Hey, Give me my coat back!"

I started giggling and Grandma snatched the picture from my hands. She looked at it and then to my horror she gave it to Mama. Mama looked at the picture and then glared at Vickie and then me. She showed the picture to Daddy who simply looked at it and put it in his suit pocket. Both my parent's faces went blank and I saw Mama's jaw start to grind. For the rest of the service, Vickie and I sat stone still.

When service finally ended we all stood up and began to file out. When we got to the foyer, Mr. Roy and Mr. Al were waiting for Mama and Daddy. I could tell already that I was probably going to get a spanking when we got home, but I tried to be brave. Mr. Roy and Mr. Al related everything that had happened in class that morning. Mama and Daddy thanked them and said they were going to have a talk with me when we got home. I was sure there wouldn't be talking though.

We got to the car, and Vickie and I sat miserably in the back seat. We drove to our neighborhood and stopped in front of Mr. Kemp's house. Mama turned around and said,

"Tonya scoot over and make room for Mr. Kemp." He is coming to our house for Sunday dinner."

I couldn't believe it! Mama and Daddy didn't love me after all and were letting a wife beater sit next to me in the car. Vickie sort of scooted way over to give me plenty of room. I watched in disbelief when Daddy got out of the car, rang Mr. Kemp's doorbell, and shook Mr. Kemp's hand. He led Mr. Kemp to the car and Mr. Kemp sat down next to me. I was terrified.

Mama turned and introduced us.

"Mr. Kemp, these are my children Vickie, Tonya and Rebecca is up here with me."

"Nice to meet you," said creepy Mr. Kemp.

"Nice to meet you too," I heard myself say.

Daddy got in the front seat and winked at me in the rearview mirror. I understood that this was my punishment and didn't need to fear a spanking. I was relieved for about two seconds until I remembered that Mr. Kemp was centimeters away. We drove the short distance back to our house which seemed like it took hours. When we pulled into the drive, Mama said,

"You girls go in and get changed, and then you can help me finish the rest of dinner."

Vickie and I changed into our play clothes and hung our Sunday dresses up in the closet. Mama's rule was you only wore your Sunday dress for a few hours, so you could hang it up until it had been worn for two Sundays. I put on my pink tennis shoes and wondered what was going to happen next. Vickie and I went to the kitchen to help Mama. Of course, I was stuck making the salad again and Vickie made the sweet tea. Rebecca set the table and then she and I had to get the piano bench so we would have somewhere to sit at the table.

Daddy and Mr. Kemp were in the family room building a fire and talking about football. Our poodle Tiffany was warily sniffing at Mr. Kemp. I always said Tiffany was a good judge of character because she always tried to bite our neighborhood bully, Brad. Apparently Tiffany didn't care for Mr. Kemp either because she was growling. Daddy commanded "Quiet, Tiff!" and Tiffany came next to me in the kitchen. Tiffany liked me best because I gave her liver under the table when Mama cooked it. Also I loved Tiffany and talked and patted her almost constantly.

Vickie, Rebecca, and I must have been awkwardly quiet because Mama kept trying to make conversation. She took the chicken and rice out of the oven and put it on the table. I put the salad and the cucumbers in vinegar on the table. Rebecca and Vickie both had to put all the salad dressing on the table.

Cheri's Daddy was a salesperson for Wish Bone brand foods, so he gave us free sample of all the new salad dressings. At any given time, we would have at least eight bottles of dressing. Mama instructed us to put two bottles at each corner so everyone could view the possibilities. I always put the Thousand Island between Mama and me. Daddy liked the French. Rebecca liked the Catalina and

Vickie liked the Ranch. The other weird flavors like Green Goddess, Vinaigrette, Cheesy Dip, and the rest were put anywhere on the table.

Mama told me and Rebecca to sit on the bench and Mr. Kemp sat down next to Vickie. I smiled at her across the table and received a kick under it. We all sat down. Daddy asked who would like to say the prayer. Daddy's philosophy was that everyone should have the opportunity to lead prayers even if they were girls. No one volunteered so Daddy said,

"Tonya, you need some extra practice this morning so you do it."

Again the feeling of Daddy betraying me made me blush. He knew I couldn't refuse and so I sighed and began,

"Dear God in Heaven, thank you for the food we are about to eat. Thank you for your son who died on the cross for our sins, and thank you for our special guest Mr. Kemp. In Jesus' name we pray, Amen."

I had decided to stick with the standard stuff instead of what I was really thinking. The whole time I was praying, I was keeping a watchful eye on Mr. Kemp; afraid he may jump up and stab us all. Vickie was sneaking peeks as well but it was Rebecca who ratted us out. When I was done Rebecca pointed at me and Vickie and said,

"Daddy, they were lookin' during the prayer."

Daddy just replied, "How do you know if your eyes were closed?"

Poor dumb little Rebecca said, "Because I saw them."

Mr. Kemp sort of snorted and so did Daddy.

"Mr. Kemp, which part of the chicken would you like?" Mama asked sweetly.

"I believe I would like the wishbone please," he replied.

This made me mad. Everyone knew that was Mama's favorite piece and now he had taken it. Of course, Mama simply dished it out with a big helping of rice too. What happened next shocked Vickie and I so much we almost choked. Little Rebecca pointed at Mr. Kemp's plate and sort of shouted, "Mr. Kemp took Mama's piece! You better give it back!" Little Rebeccca was never mad so this was surprising.

"It's alright Rebecca; I'll just have a different piece." Mama's face flushed red from embarrassment. Mr. Kemp turned to Mama,

" It's nice your girls stand up for you. If you don't mind I'd like to change to one of those thighs."

"I won't hear it," Mama said politely.

Mama took one of the thigh pieces and some rice. She gave Daddy the back and Rebecca leg. Vickie chose her piece, and I was last. I guess that was just another piece of my punishment for what had happened in Bible class. I knew it was just best to keep my mouth shut and ride it out.

After everyone was served and eating, Daddy began what seemed like light conversation. At our house it was the rule to only have pleasant conversation at the table so everyone could digest properly. Daddy asked Mr. Kemp, "How are things in the air conditioning business?"

"Good, of course not as good as in the summer. We do heating too, so we are always busy."

I wasn't paying much attention to the conversation because I was watching Vickie across the table. Never before had I seen terror in her eyes, like I did now. Vickie had successfully slid her chair over about two inches away from Mr. Kemp and hadn't eaten a bite. The latter was of greater importance because Vickie was a bottomless pit. Even though she was skinny, Vickie could out eat any teenage boy. Daddy used to thump on her leg to see if it was hollow. Today though, Vickie's appetite had taken a vacation.

As I watched Vickie scoot further away from Mr. Kemp I noticed something else. Mr. Kemp was wearing his wedding ring. To me this was odd for two reasons. First, I had never seen a man wear jewelry before because Daddy couldn't wear his ring at the shop, and second, well, Mrs. Kemp was dead. For some reason this made me a little sad but I didn't know why. My face must have given me away, because Daddy caught me off guard.

"What are you thinking about?" he asked.

I blurted out, "Oh, I was just looking at Mr. Kemp's ring."

Mr. Kemp looked at me dead in the eye.

"You know some people have asked why I still wear it."

"Well, that's none of our business," Mama cut in.

"Oh, it's all right Mrs. Agnew. I'll tell you why. You see I love Mrs. Kemp and even though she's gone I want to remember the happy times we had together."

There was an uncomfortable silence until little Rebecca, God bless her, asked,

"Where'd she go?"

"She went to live with the angels in heaven," said Mr. Kemp.

Vickie and I exchanged looks and I knew she was thinking about the vote we had taken.

"Is she an angel now?" asked Rebecca.

"I don't know, but I know she surely was one here on earth," replied Mr. Kemp.

Vickie and I looked at Mama who was fighting back tears.

"Mama, can I have some more rice?" I was trying to save Mama.

"As soon as you are finished with your first serving," Mama choked out.

After that the conversation turned to other things like Daddy's work and the upcoming Christmas holiday. Mama wanted to know what Mr. Kemp's plans were and he said he was going to visit his brother and his family in Dallas.

Once dinner was finished and Mama had served us pecan pie for dessert, Daddy and Mr. Kemp watched some football and Vickie and I helped Mama with the dishes. Rebecca sat on Daddy's lap and cheered whenever Daddy and Mr. Kemp cheered. When the Cowboys won again Mr. Kemp stood up to go home. He thanked Mama and turned to Vickie and me.

"I want to thank you girls for letting me come over today." His eyes were looking sad again.

I managed a "Thank you for coming," and then Daddy said he was going to walk Mr. Kemp home. I walked to the front door and opened it just in time for my friend Cheri to ring the doorbell. When she looked up and saw who was coming out of our house she just stood there dumbstruck. Daddy excused himself and then he and Mr. Kemp began walking slowly down the sidewalk. I turned around and noticed Mama wasn't looking so I motioned for Cheri to follow.

We followed Daddy and Mr. Kemp about two houses behind. When they got to Mr. Kemp's house they shook hands and Mr. Kemp went inside. The next thing I saw was the most shocking sight I had ever seen. Daddy sniffed really loud and then wiped his eyes. Daddy was crying! This was too much. I ran to him and hugged him really tight. He looked down and smiled but he didn't say anything to me or Cheri the whole walk home.

CHAPTER 7

Gifts

*T*he last day of school before Christmas break was my favorite day at school. This was the day the room mothers arranged for a Christmas party for the class. Mama always helped by baking some cookies or brownies and I took these to school with me along with the small gift Mama had purchased for Mrs. Reed. I told Mama that Mrs. Reed probably wouldn't like whatever I brought so to try to hide who brought it I just wrote my initial on the tag. I figured this way maybe Mrs. Reed would have to say she liked it before she figured out who it was from. Mama always bought our teachers gifts even though we didn't have much money. I wondered if that was why Mama had taken that extra job gift wrapping at nights. Sometimes I couldn't figure out Mama.

In addition to giving a present to the teacher, we also bought a small gift for a girl or boy in the class. I was always excited to see the reaction of the person I bought for. I almost always gave a book because I loved to read and some of my favorites always ended up as a gift. I'll admit that I gave some of my own copies away because I wanted someone else to enjoy the book as much as me. This year I was giving away "Pyewacket". It was the story of some cats that took over their street. I had even marked my favorite parts with pencil so whoever got it could enjoy those parts too. Mama tried to get me to buy something new, but I was insistent. Boy, how I wished I had listened to Mama.

Of course there wasn't much teaching or learning on this day and in fact, most of it was spent making snow-flakes, snowmen, Santa Clause and snowy cabin pictures made from cotton balls and glitter. Weeks before, we had made advent calendars counting down the days until Christmas. There was one exception though. My friend Joanna was Jewish so she didn't make an advent calendar on account of it counting down to Jesus' birthday.

The morning of the party our class was also perform-ing a sort of play about Christmas. I got to be one of the angels at Jesus' manger. I had to kneel and put my hands together like I was praying while the rest of the third grade sang "Away in a Manger". Mrs. Echols, the music teacher, lead with passion, but everybody cheered loudest when a tall kid named Randy came out dressed as Rudolph the Red Nosed Reindeer. His costume was great! It had a giant head with a blinking red nose. After the play, we all headed back to Mrs. Reed's room for cookies, brownies, and just about every kind of sugary treat imaginable. Then came the moment of truth.

We all sat in a circle with our gifts and waited. Each gift was given a number. Next, Mrs. Reed had each child draw a number one at a time and the person with the corresponding number would stand up, give their gift to the person and say "Merry Christmas!" The receiver would say "Thank You!" and unwrap their gift while everyone watched.

Finally Darla Hanshaw drew my number. This was great because Darla was the most popular girl in the third grade and I knew she would like my gift. All eyes were on Darla as she unwrapped "Pyewacket". A queer look came over her face as she stated,

"This isn't anything but a crummy book. And look, she wrote all in it!"

Mrs. Reed looked at the book and asked,

"Tonya, don't you have some other gift for Darla?"

"No Ma'am" I muttered feeling about two inches tall.

"Well, let's move on!" dismissed Mrs. Reed.

Eventually it came down to my turn and of course I drew Darla's number. When she gave her present to me she kind of mumbled "Merry Christmas." I sheepishly said, "Thank you." When I opened the gift I thought I would die. Darla had given me the newest Barbie; Beach Barbie with <u>two</u> swimsuits. All the girls ooohed and aaahed but when I looked at Darla she stuck her tongue out at me.

After everyone had been given a gift, we all got ready to go home. Mrs. Reed called me and Darla to her desk.

"Tonya, Darla, I think we better talk about the gifts. Tonya what do you have to say?"

"Mrs. Reed, that was my favorite book and I wanted whoever got it to like it as much as I did, so I underlined all the good parts." I explained.

"Well, Darla what about you?"

"Everyone loves Barbies," was all she said.

"Let's do this," said Mrs. Reed. "Tonya, you take your book and Darla you keep the Barbie and we'll call it even."

I was too humiliated to point out that it wasn't even so I just shook my head okay. Darla smirked at me and said she was okay with that. Mrs. Reed said that Darla could go get ready to go home but she wanted to speak with me privately. I thought I was in for it. Mrs. Reed began,

"Tonya, I wanted to say thank you for the nice candle you gave me for Christmas. I also think that what you were trying to do with the book was nice, but I want you to remember two things. First, you must never write in books, and second only new gifts are best."

At that moment I had my first violent thought about a teacher. I wanted to punch Mrs. Reed in the mouth. However, I had a better plan so I simply said "Yes, Ma'am," and got ready to go home. All the way home I knew what I was going to do to exact my revenge on Mrs. Reed. As soon as I got home, I went straight to my room, knelt by the bed and prayed,

"Dear God,

I am really mad at Mrs. Reed and I need your help! I don't ever pray for mean things, Dear God, but you and I know Mrs. Reed is just plain black-hearted. So Lord, please make that nice candle Mama gave her catch her house on fire and burn it down! In Jesus' name I pray AMEN!"

I never felt as good as I did that moment. I had been taught that if God was on your side, you won. I put "Pyewacket" back on my shelf and began doing the chores Mama asked me to do. When I was done, Mama asked how school was. I told her only what she needed to know and waited.

I waited for the six o'clock news. I just knew there would be a report of a local third grade teacher's house burning to the ground. I sort of waited feverishly through supper and then I sat next to Daddy while he watched. All the usual stuff about Vietnam, and the weather was on and finally after thirty minutes, the news was over. I couldn't believe it. Then I thought that maybe Mrs. Reed would wait and light that candle when it got dark and then the report would be on the ten o'clock news. I was really looking forward to that newscast.

Since it was the last day of school and I didn't have any homework, Mama let me help her in the kitchen. Mama had begun her Christmas baskets for the neighbors and she needed help with some assembly. Mama always baked treats for the neighbors because it was inexpensive and she knew all the other ladies would be giving something to us. Mama's banana nut bread and homemade fruit cake were the favorites of all our neighbors. Mama's fruit cake was supposedly the best because she made it at Thanksgiving and let it "age" on top of the refrigerator for two or three weeks.

I found out later that the real reason it tasted so good, was that somehow Daddy had a connection with one of the owners of a liquor store. Since our county was a dry county, several liquor stores had built a sort of liquor mall on the county line which was called "The Strip". The Strip wasn't too far from our house. Daddy was able to get the best brand of the particular kind of liquor Mama put in her fruit cake for free. I didn't find this out until I was about seventeen years old and allowed to taste Mama's fruit cake for the first time. I was allowed because there was a deal between my parents and me.

The deal was, I wouldn't tell about seeing one of our church leaders coming out of the liquor store and my parents wouldn't take my car I had been drag racing at the time, and I could have my first taste of alcohol in their presence. I remember vividly feeling so grown up having alcohol with my parents, but a little miffed when I found out it would be in fruit cake form. To this day I despise fruit cake.

Anyway, Mama had finished the baking and so she had the baskets lined up and ready to fill. Mama gave me two baskets with a list for each one that said what particular treats and how many of each went inside. I got the

Campbell's and to my surprise Mr. Kemp's basket. It was a little sad, because Mr. Kemp's basket was small. I started putting the pralines, peanut butter cookies, chocolate cookies, and of course the fruit cake in Mr. Kemp's basket. My mind was ticking again.

"Mama, isn't Mr. Kemp going away for Christmas?"

"Yes, but I think he would appreciate being thought of during the holidays."

I began imagining Mr. Kemp sitting in a chair in front of Mrs. Kemp's picture eating Mama's fruit caked humming "Jingle Bells" really slowly. I shuddered and wondered how I could have such a creepy mind sometimes. Of course it was just a momentary thought because Mama began making small talk and filling the baskets. Vickie came into the kitchen and sort of half-heartedly began helping. Vickie knew she needed to be a little helpful close to Christmas just like every kid does. Vickie was putting together the Borgers' basket and asked, "Mama, do I hafta help deliver this year?"

"Don't you want to?"

"Mama, I'm getting too old and Tonya can take Rebecca with her."

"That's a good idea," said Mama.

I knew Vickie was just getting out of doing work, but Mama was right. I could take Rebecca and she would surely just eat up all the compliments the neighbors gave. Mama always had us girls deliver the baskets in our new Christmas dresses because that way we could wear the dresses as much as possible. She said it gave us good practice with Christian charity too.

"Mama, I'll do it with Rebecca," I said.

I wanted to be in charge of something. Vickie looked sideways at me and crooned,

"Even Mr. Kemp's?"

"Sure! " I said breezily.

"Just don't let him get ya!" laughed Vickie.

"Cut it out Vickie. I thought we had cleared all that up."

I loved it when Vickie got in trouble. Vickie got her last shot in though as she continued putting treats in the basket.

"What did you get at your class party today?" she asked as if she didn't already know everything.

I was silent but shot Vickie a dirty look. She must have heard about it from someone. I had two choices. I could lie or just tell the truth. I thought for a second and thought about what I had prayed for. I figured lying might change God's mind about my request, so I told the truth.

Mama listened and kept working. I told Mama everything including what Mrs. Reed told me about books and presents. Mama sighed really deep and asked,

"Honey, what do you think about what Mrs. Reed said?"

"Well, I think she is a mean old lady who doesn't like me," I said.

"But that wasn't my question. What do you think about what she said about books and presents?"

I thought for just long enough and said,

"Mama, I think writing in books is good because it helps you remember stuff, but I think she may be right about new presents."

"So what about these baskets we are putting together for the neighbors? I mean, I used flour, eggs, spices, cookie sheets, and the baskets are from last year, so does that make my gift not good enough?"

I loved my Mama so much at that moment. She continued,

"Honey, you write in every book you want to from now on. Don't listen to people who are so materialistic they can't see the love in a gift."

I didn't know what she meant by materialistic, but I knew enough that she was calling Mrs. Reed wrong. I felt like I should tell mama about the prayer, so I did. Her reaction was not what I expected. She laughed so hard she started crying. Daddy came to the kitchen to see what was going on. Mama told him and Daddy quoted quite seriously,

"Out of the mouths of babes," and "Vengeance is mind sayeth the Lord".

Mama and Daddy were really strange with their humor. After a few minutes Mama composed herself and explained,

"Honey, things like that don't work that way. I'm sure the good Lord has lots of other things to take care of. Besides, you don't really want that to happen to Mrs. Reed do you?"

"No, not really Mama, but I was mad."

"Well, I wouldn't worry. God knows how you feel and He does what is best. Let's finish these up; you and Rebecca deliver them tomorrow."

I had a different prayer that night. I thanked God for Mama and Daddy and really meant it.

Pancakes and a Special Request

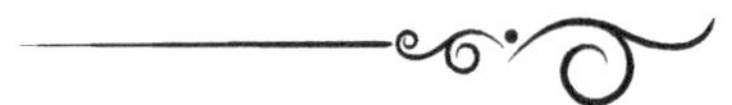

The next morning I woke up freezing. A cold front had come in and our old gas heater was only set to 68 degrees, but it felt colder than that. I looked over at Vickie who was buried under her covers. I got out of bed and made my way to the kitchen. I was the first one up and when I looked at the clock it said 6am. I guessed that I got too cold and woke up. I went to Mama and Daddy's room and whispered,

"It's cold".

Daddy stirred and opened one eye. He put his finger to his lips and pointed at Mama and then shimmied out of bed. He shivered and went straight for the thermostat. Our old heater kicked in with its weird sputtering noises that sounded like footsteps coming down the hall. That old heater was just plain creepy at night when the pilot was trying to light the burners. You would swear that someone was walking slowly down the hall getting faster and faster until the burners lit with a whoosh. Vickie and I used to scare each other pretending it was a monster or a burglar.

Daddy went to the kitchen and began making the coffee so it would be ready when Mama got up. I huddled on the couch. Finally, he half whispered,

"Why don't you get dressed really quietly and we'll go to the Pancake House."

As quickly and quietly as I could, I dressed. Going to the Pancake House was a treat. I liked it too that just Daddy and I were going because sometimes he would let me order coffee. We got in the truck and started towards downtown.

It was quiet in the morning especially Saturdays. We drove past the cotton field that was empty and lay fallow before spring planting. Our neighborhood was bordered by the high school football stadium, the loop around town, and 66th street. Since it was close to Christmas, some of the yards had various decorations. I was looking forward to Christmas and all the presents. I was thinking about all this when Daddy broke the silence.

"You're sure quiet this morning, whatcha' thinking about."

"Christmas."

"Really? When is that?"

"Very funny, Daddy."

"So what do you want for Christmas?"

I had been waiting for this question for a long time and knew exactly what to say.

"Daddy, I want a rabbit coat. All the girls at school have one and I'd just love one."

Daddy looked surprised. I think he was shocked to find out that his fishing buddy and assistant mechanic was turning into a girl.

"Well honey, that sound nice, but if all the other girls were getting say...a...shotgun would you want that too?"

"Heck, yeah!" I chimed.

Daddy was relieved that I wasn't all the way girl yet because he grinned and chuckled.

"What I mean is, is the only reason you want it is because everyone else has one?"

I could spot a loaded question a mile away, but this one was truly difficult to answer. I said nothing.

"That's my girl. If you can't answer right away that means that question is worth a second think."

Just about then we pulled into the Pancake House Restaurant. The Pancake House was an old building then, but they always had a steady stream of patrons. Mostly, it was truckers, or farmers who were up super early and hungry for breakfast by 6:30am. Inside the whole place smelled like bacon; lots and lots of bacon. It was the kind of smell that made the air heavy, but warm and comforting. The place was packed.

Daddy nodded familiarly to some of the truck drivers and farmers. A few of them knew me from past visits as well and made remarks like,

"Well, hello there little lady!" or "Got your helper today I see." or "Who's your girlfriend?"

I don't know why it made me feel weird and shy when they said that but every time, I blushed and looked at the floor.

The same waitress we had every time came to our table. Daddy always called her that "purdy little redhead gal" even though she must have been pushing sixty. Her name was Miss Mary.

"Good morning, John!"

"Good morning, Miss Mary".

Why he called her Miss Mary was a mystery to me.

"I bet Miss Tonya would like the Silver Dollar Special with bacon on the side fried crisp not flimsy."

Miss Mary knew that's all I ever ordered. I was fascinated by those tiny pancakes.

"That's right!" I chirped.

"Are you having coffee this morning?" Miss Mary winked at Daddy.

"Can I Daddy? Pleeeeease?"

"Now you know that stunts your growth and makes hair grow on your chest. I think maybe half a cup with the other half warm milk would be alright. I'll have my usual Peanut Butter Pancakes and coffee."

"Sure thing, honey." It was weird that Miss Mary flirted with Daddy.

"Daddy, why doesn't Mama have hair on her chest since she drinks coffee every day?"

"She does, but she spends at least an hour every morning plucking them out," he joked.

I laughed and laughed at the visual in my head. While we waited for our food I asked Daddy my own loaded question.

"Daddy, what do you want for Christmas?" I already knew his pat answer.

"Nothing, I already have everything I need."

"Okay, but if you could get anything your wanted, even if it wasn't something you needed what would it be?"

"You know you're a smart cookie. I guess there are a couple of things. Let's see...binoculars, a new fishing pole, a Swiss Army knife, a new truck, some warm socks, a new hat, some work boots, warm socks, a new socket wrench set, a new Coleman stove, a new Coleman lantern, did I say warm socks? I guess that's about it."

"Holy cow Daddy! Your list is longer than mine."

"Well you said anything."

Miss Mary brought our breakfast and we ate almost in silence. I drank my coffee with milk and sugar. We left Miss Mary a nice tip and she gave me a quick hug and a Merry Christmas. She just winked at Daddy. We drove home and went in as quietly as possible in case no one else was up. As we got to the kitchen Rebecca squealed,

"I'm ready!"

Apparently, Rebecca was so excited about delivering the Christmas baskets with me; she had gotten up, put on her dress, and attempted to brush her own hair. She was just too darn cute. At some point she couldn't get one of the tangles out so she just left the comb dangling in her hair. Her dress was on backwards so she could button it up by herself, and her shoes were on the wrong feet.

"Rebecca, it's too early. Let's wait until about 2 o'clock. People wouldn't like it if we woke them up. Let's go find you some play clothes until then."

I think dealing diplomatically with Rebecca helped prepare me for my own children later. I picked out Rebecca's outfit and poured her a bowl of Cocoa Puffs.

Mama woke up at about 8:30 that morning which for her was early for a Saturday. I knew she was getting ready to do some last minute Christmas shopping. Mama had her coffee, showered, dressed and told Daddy she was going. The stores were only going to be open from 10 am to 4pm that day and Mama had to do her gift wrapping job from 2-4pm, so she wanted to leave and go straight to the job when she was finished shopping.

Mama left us a list of chores to be done while she was gone, so I started right away. I knew if I finished, I could go to Cheri's house to play. I picked up all my clothes, did the dishes, and was ready to go.

"Daddy, I am going to Cheri's!"

"Hang on, take Rebecca with you."

"Oh Daddy, do I have to?"

"Well she either goes or you both stay home."

"Come on, Rebecca." I moped.

This was great news to Rebecca. She got to hang out with her big sister. As we walked to Cheri's we had to pass the alley where the fence came so close to the sidewalk you couldn't see around it. Rebecca stopped.

"I'm scared."

"Okay, I'll count to three then we'll run across together. Give me your hand."

When I hit three, we tore out. Since she was younger she couldn't go as fast as I wanted her to. I didn't want to let on that I was scared of that alley too, but when we safely reached the other side, I was breathing deep breaths of relief.

When we got to Cheri's house I rang the bell. Cheri's older brother Michael answered the door. I had a huge crush on Michael and thought he was gorgeous. He wasn't interested in me though since he was already in junior high school and I was just a little kid. He knew I had a crush on him though and kind of egged me on.

"Cheri, your cute little friend is here!" he called.

I blushed a deep red. When Cheri saw that Rebecca was with me, she threw up her hands.

"Sorry, Daddy made me bring her," I apologized.

"Cheri, can we play with your Barbies?" Rebecca asked hopefully.

"I guess so," Cheri replied gloomily.

We went to Cheri's room and began dressing all the Barbies. Rebecca had the fashion sense of a three year old, which irked Cheri to no end.

"You can't put pink boots with green pants. It's tacky."

"But those are my favorite colors, and I want Barbie to look pretty, "Rebecca wailed.

This argument went on forever until Rebecca stopped playing and started pouting. Both Rebecca and Cheri were the youngest of the family, and both were used to getting their way. I guess that's why they didn't get along very well. Cheri's Mama came in and told her it was time for me and Rebecca to go home. Again, we ran past the alley and when we got home Daddy was working on the truck.

"Did y'all have fun?"

"I guess."

"Well now don't get too excited."

"We were just playing, that's all."

"Well, do you want to help me fix the radiator?"

"No, I'm just going to ride my bike around the block, okay?"

"Alright, be back soon so you can deliver those baskets, okay?"

I went inside and turned on cartoons for Rebecca. I got my bike out of the garage. I rode past Mrs. White's house and began thinking about everything that had happened since Halloween. The next thing I knew I was in front of Mr. Kemp's house just staring at it. I was thinking about Mr. Kemp being all alone at Christmas when suddenly a tear ran down my face. Then for no reason I was bawling! I couldn't believe it. I was really turning into a girl.

"Are you okay?"

I looked up and realized that at some point Mr. Kemp had seen me and was now standing in front of this crazy crying baby. I don't know what possessed me, but I began blurting out everything. I mean everything. I told him how the neighbors had heard him talking to Mrs. Kemp's portrait, about how some said he beat Mrs. Kemp, and about how some said his house was haunted by her ghost, about how all the kids thought he was creepy, and I just kept going and going. It was like a dam had burst and all my thoughts just gushed out. Finally, I stopped and looked at Mr. Kemp who had heard every word. He was kind of giggling. I was furious.

"Are you making fun of me?"

"No, I'm just kind of relieved to hear why no one will speak to me, other than your parents of course. They all think I am a terrible man, huh?"

"I guess so."

"Well thank you for telling me. I want you to do something for me. Will you?"

"I guess it depends on what it is." I replied.

"Your Daddy was right, you are a smart one. Listen, all I want you to do is pass out some invitations for me. I am going to have a sort of a celebration and I want all the neighbors and their families to come."

"Okay, I can do that when I deliver the baskets for Mama."

"Great! Did your Mama make her delicious fruit cake?"

"Yes sir, me and Rebecca will deliver the baskets later this afternoon."

"I'll see you then. Let me get the invitations. Wait right here," he smiled and went inside.

I sniffed and wondered what the heck I was doing. My life was getting weirder and weirder by the minute. I had cried in front of a man I barely knew, spilled the beans about the neighbors, and agreed to deliver some message of doom from a wife beater. All I could think about was what other weirdness might happen at Mr. Kemp's "celebration". Maybe he would have a piñata that looked like Mrs. Kemp that all the guests would beat up just like he used to. Maybe he would hang it in the garage in the same spot Mrs. Kemp hung herself. I was totally letting my imagination go crazy.

When I got home, to my surprise, Mama had come back home. She said she had just needed to pick something up from one of the stores and she had time enough to come home and do a couple of chores before going to her gift wrapping job. Mama went to her room and closed the door which meant she was wrapping gifts.

I asked when she came out,

"Mama, me and Rebecca are ready to deliver the baskets now if it isn't still too early."

"All right, go put on your Christmas dress and I'll get Rebecca ready."

"Wait Mama, there's something I need to tell you. I was in front of Mr. Kemp's house and he asked me to deliver these invitations with our baskets."

"What were you doing down there? Let me see those."

Mama took the invitations and opened the one that was marked for us. It read:

Dear neighbors,

Please join me on December 23rd at my house for snacks, drinks, and a good time. Please come at 7:00pm.

Thank you, Kemp

"Well, this is a surprise."

"I told Mr. Kemp I would deliver them."

"Then that's what you'll do. This means that his party is tomorrow night after church so we can go."

I thought Mama must be losing her mind. Still I was curious about seeing that portrait of Mrs. Kemp in real life. Also, since Cheri's family was invited she would be there too. Vickie came in just long enough to tease me and then left to play football. Rebecca and I loaded the baskets into her little wagon and I rehearsed with her what to say.

"All right, Rebecca, when we get to each house, we ring the doorbell and then when they answer we say 'Merry Christmas from our family to yours!'

First we went next door and when Mrs. Boyter answered Rebecca recited her lines perfectly and handed Mrs. Boyter her basket. I gave her Mr. Kemp's invitation.

"Thank you and Merry Christmas to you too. Now here is something for your family too."

She handed me a small package. Rebecca's eyes lit up. I had forgotten to tell her that the neighbors would probably give us presents too. We continued down the block until once again I was in front of Mr. Kemp's house.

"I don't want to do this house. I'm scared." Rebecca whined.

"It's just Mr. Kemp. I'm right here with you."

We rang the bell and Mr. Kemp answered.

"Hello ladies, don't y'all look pretty today!"

"Merry Christmas from our family to yours." Rebecca kind of half whispered.

"Thank you, and here is something for your family. Have you been delivering the invitations?"

"Yes sir."

"Good, I hope at least some people come." Mr. Kemp sounded nervous.

"Well, Mama said we are coming since it's after church."

"Oh good! If y'all come maybe some of the other neighbors will too."

"All right, we will see you tomorrow night."

"Okay, bye now."

We delivered the rest of the baskets and went home with more packages from the neighbors. Mama was on the phone when we came in.

"I think it's nice and we are going." Mama said to whoever she was talking to.

"No, it just says to be there, but I'll probably take something. I need to go now okay? All right, goodbye."

"Everyone is calling to thank us for the baskets and to ask about Mr. Kemp's invitation."

"Who all is coming?" I asked.

"Well, Cheri and her family are going so at least you'll have someone to play with."

"Good. I think she really wants to see that picture of Mrs. Kemp."

Cheri and I had talked about the painting almost daily since we had found out about it. We speculated about what Mr. Kemp said to it and even went so far as to giving Mrs. Kemp words to say in return. It was creepy to think about, which is why it was irresistible. We would sit for hours and think up conversations. My best one went like this:

> *Mr. Kemp: Well honey don't you look nice.*
>
> *Mrs. Kemp: I'll always look this good now.*
>
> *Mr. Kemp: How's the Devil?*
>
> *Mrs. Kemp: As mean as always.*
>
> *Mr. Kemp: Well tell him I said hello.*
>
> *Mrs. Kemp: Oh he's waiting for you to come tell him yourself.*
>
> *Mr. Kemp: Oh yeah, I forgot. See ya later.*
>
> *Mrs. Kemp: See you soon, soon, soon...*

Cheri always got scared on that last part which is why it was the best. I was thinking about everything that had happened when Vickie came into the kitchen with her pajamas still on.

"Morning Miss Merry Sunshine," teased Mama.

"Hey, did I hear we are going somewhere after church tomorrow?" Vickie asked dreamily.

"Yep," I said, "Mr. Kemp's house."

"Holy cow! That's far out! I can't wait to see where Mrs. Kemp hung herself!" Vickie cried.

"Oh my gosh, don't be so morbid, Vickie."

I knew how Vickie felt. Imagine how weird and creepy it would be if you actually went to the place where Mrs. Kemp died. My imagination began turning again and I thought about the rope.

"Do you think the rope is still there?"

"Tonya Kaye Agnew!"

I knew I was in for it because Mama had used all three of my names. Mama glared at me and pointed to my room. I knew that meant I would be there the rest of the day and couldn't play with Cheri or anyone. I slunk to my room, lay on the bed and took out "Charlotte's Web." I had already read it, but I liked it so much I read it seven times. Whenever I felt bad I turned to the part where Wilbur's best friend Charlotte dies. That way if I was caught crying, I could blame it on the book. I flipped to that section and sure enough felt my eyes begin to swell and flood. Why I always cried at that part was beyond me, but it always made me feel better if I shed some tears.

Mama came to see me after about half an eternity to bring me a snack and to talk. Mama had a stern look so I knew I'd better listen and not do any talking.

"Honey, what you said earlier was really wrong. I know you're a curious one, but sometimes you go too far. You shouldn't be thinking about death at such a young age and I'm worried you are turning out to be too morbid."

I didn't know what morbid meant so I asked.

"It is being too concerned or thinking too much about death. If you are morbid, you can't enjoy the good things in life. Now you are going to stay here until supper I think."

Mama handed me a piece of paper and a pen.

"You are going to write 100 times 'Life is good and I am truly blessed' on this paper and then maybe you will think about the good in your life."

I hated writing punishments. I hated having to write what I didn't want to, and it didn't help that I am left handed and the pen always smears on my hand. Mama saw me roll my eyes.

"You are being punished so deal with it."

Mama left and I began writing. I went to sit at the antique school desk my Uncle had given me. I always felt like I was a serious student when I sat in it, and I tried to imagine what school was like a long time ago. I started writing and remembered a trick dreamy Sean had showed me at school. Sean was always having to write lines for one thing or another and he showed me a way to kind of cheat at it. The trick was to write whatever the first word was 100 times down the left margin. Then you wrote the second word and so on. When you were done, the paper had neat rows of words and Sean had explained that the reason this punishment was given in the first place was to improve neatness. I thought Sean was so clever, and gorgeous.

I wrote the word Life 100 times and all I could think about was Mrs. Kemp hanging in the garage. At some point while I was writing "is", my snack must have made me sleepy because my mind wandered and I thought about what Mrs. Kemp must have looked like when they found her. I had a vision that her face was purple and her eyes were kind of bugged out. Just as I got to really envisioning her face clearly, Mrs. Kemp looked at me and yelled,

"Gotcha!"

I jumped out of my skin and realized it was Vickie who had scared me. I was furious, but crafty.

"Mama," I wailed and stirred up some tears.

"Shut up, shut up, shut up I was only kidding."

Mama came in and saw two things: my tears and my work.

"Good Lord! You girls are driving me crazy. Vickie, leave her alone and Tonya you start your work over again!"

Vickie and I looked at each other and kind of winked. We knew most of the time Mama was mostly hot air, so when she got mad at us, if we egged her on a little we could get her so say something really funny.

"Mama, why is writing a punishment?"

"Tonya Kaye, you are about to pull the last thread out of my dress!"

After Mama left Vickie and I laughed and laughed. Mama was hilarious when she got flustered. Vickie waited until Mama was out of earshot.

"Hey, I have a plan so we can get into that garage and see where Mrs. Kemp killed herself. We are going to use Rebecca as a distraction. You know how people think she is so cute, right? Well, we're going to have her start singing some Christmas song and when all the adults are listening to her we will sneak into the garage with this."

Vickie pulled out the old Brownie our Grandpa had given her. He was an amateur photographer, and when Vickie asked for it, he showed her how to use it. Vickie had taken some neat pictures of our dog, Tiffany, and considered herself a pro. Our plan was getting bigger.

"I'm going to stand on something and point to where she was hanging."

My imagination was really working overtime now. Vickie and I were giddy. Rebecca came into our room.

"Hey Rebecca, do you know the song the Twelve Days of Christmas?"

"Yeah, we sing it at preschool. It helps us learn numbers. I can sing it now, 'On the fwurst day of Cwissmas my twue wub gabe to mee, a pawtridge in a pwear twee...'

This was going to be great. People would think it was so cute the way Rebecca pronounced things, and that song lasts forever and a day, so it would give us plenty of time to get the picture. Vickie and I gave each other a thumbs up, but Rebecca thought we meant to sing louder. She continued almost yelling,

"ON THE SEQUAND DAY OF CHWISSMAS MY TWUE WUB GABE TO ME, TWO TWURTLE DOVES"

Mama came in.

"Vickie, and Rebecca, Tonya is being punished so you have to leave her alone. Tonya get to writing!"

"Mama, I forgot what I was supposed to write," I lied.

Apparently Mama had forgotten to so she looked at my paper with 100 Life's on it and said,

"I think it was 'Life is good'".

I had successfully cut my work in half. When I was done it was time for supper. Mama had decided on what she called "mustgo". Basically, it was all the leftovers in the refrigerator from the week. This was great because there might be pancakes, roast, chicken, pork chops, salad, scrambled eggs, and whatever else. It was like getting your favorites all in one dinner. I wasn't paying much attention but perked my ears up.

"Honey, tomorrow after church Mr. Kemp is having a get together for the neighbors."

"Really? That's interesting. Have you and the other hens on the street decided that the wolf won't eat you if you go?"

Mama laughed.

"Well, some feathers are ruffled, but I have convinced them that it could actually be fun."

Mama and Daddy discussed the particulars and supper ended.

"Tonya, and Vickie, you two will be doing dishes so you can wash any funny ideas out of your heads too. "

Vickie and I just got to clearing the table and doing dishes since we wanted to talk about our plan. We waited until Mama and Daddy had gone into the family room to watch "HeeHaw". Daddy called it his educational television. Mama didn't like it because the jokes were corny and stupid, but Daddy thought that was the best part. I liked it because of the music.

Vickie was washing and I was drying, and Rebecca was stacking the dishes. Vickie and I kept our voices low so Mama and Daddy wouldn't hear.

"Rebecca, I think tomorrow night, you should sing for everybody at the party, don't you?" Vickie prodded.

"Okay,"

Rebecca loved attention and would always try to find ways to get it. Step one of our plan was complete. After the dishes were done, our hair rolled, and we were in bed, Vickie and I continued our scheming.

"We have to have plan B, so in case something happens and Rebecca gets too scared to sing or something," said Vickie.

Sometimes it was useful having an older sister who knew about those kinds of things.

"How about asking Mrs. Campbell to sing? She sings in her choir at church and loves attention as much as Rebecca."

"Yeah, maybe that way everyone will join in and no one will ever think about us."

Plan B was complete and Vickie and I settled in for the night.

CHAPTER 9

The Party

The next morning in Bible class we talked about giving to God. I knew this was just a way to keep us kids from being greedy about our Christmas presents. I made sure to say all the right things in class, so I wouldn't get in trouble. I also made sure not to request for prayers for anyone although I secretly prayed for me and Vickie's safety as we carried out our plan. I picked up Rebecca and again we sat with Grandma and Grandpa. I sat between them so I got to hear Grandpa sing his favorite hymn, "I Surrender All" which had a tenor solo part that he sang loudly, and strongly. I looked up at him and Grandpa winked at me.

When we had prayers, Grandpa held my hand. I liked to trace the blues veins on his hand like I was tracing a road on a map. Sometimes, Grandpa would take off his Timex and let me wear it. This watch was the one he got when he worked for the Employment Commission. There are a lot of things I don't know about my Grandpa, but I do know the following:

He had been a teacher.

He sang really well.

He wrote poetry.

He loved photography.

He golfed.

He was a great story teller.

He was a Christian.

He smoked a pipe.

He drank coffee from a saucer.

He loved Grandma even though they argued.

Our preacher, Mr. Roberts, was giving a sermon about giving so when the collection plate was passed; I saw that Grandma's check was for five dollars and fifty cents. She must have felt the pressure of giving more, but Grandma had been a teenager during the Great Depression, so sometimes she worried that her money wasn't being spent right by the people in charge.

After church and Sunday dinner, Mama started working on the Lemon Merengue pie she planned to take to Mr. Kemp's party. She was worried that it was too summery a dessert for a Christmas party, but she thought it might be a welcome change. Also, it was cheap and easy to make. Vickie and I got our clothes ready and then we watched "Wild Kingdom". Mama told us we all had to have a nap because we would be up past bedtime because of the party. We all settled in and rested.

When Mama came to get me and Vickie, it was time to get ready for Sunday night church. Sunday night was different and a little more relaxed. Everyone was dressed a little more casually. Overall, I think people were just rested and ready to start a new work week. Once we got home, Mama made sure her pie looked great and touched up her wig and her make-up. Daddy changed shirts and Mama made sure all our dresses were just so.

Then it was time to go. Mama called Mrs. Campbell and all her family drove over to our house in their black station wagon. I thought their car was neat. It had been decided that we would all walk together down to Mr. Kemp's house. Mrs. Campbell made her usual comments about how good we all looked. Mama was wearing Mrs. Kemp's coat and when Mrs. Campbell noticed she remarked,

"Do you think that's a good idea?"

"Well, I don't have another coat and it's cold outside. Besides, I think Mr. Kemp won't mind."

It was a quiet walk to Mr. Kemp's house. No one seemed to have much to say. I was anticipating seeing the picture Vickie and I were going to take and about our plan to get it. I looked at Vickie who was wearing her camera around her neck. She had brought two flash cubes, so she could take eight pictures. We had certainly planned for everything.

We walked past the White's house just as they came out. The adults exchanged their hellos and handshakes and we proceeded down the block. Vickie and I filled in their daughter, Demona, in on our plan. She wanted to help. Vickie thought for a moment.

"Hey, you can be a distraction in case something goes wrong while Rebecca is singing."

"You mean like Scooby Doo and Shaggy when they are trying to catch a ghost?"

"Yeah, now I think we are really ready."

"Ready for what?" asked Daddy.

"Ready for the big Jesus lighting up thing tomorrow night."

Vickie was quick; I'll say that for sure. She must have noticed the Crawfords joining the group. Mr. Crawford would count down to zero and then plug in Baby Jesus at zero. Everyone would clap, sing "Away in a Manger" and then drink hot cocoa. It was one of the highlights of Christmas Eve.

Finally, we got to Mr. Kemp's house. We could hear Christmas music coming from inside. Daddy rang the doorbell. Mr. Kemp opened the door and exclaimed,

"Come in, come in!"

We kids were behind the grown ups and when Mr. Kemp saw me, he said,

"Well, there's my little helper," then he handed out candy canes to all of us.

When we stepped inside the first thing we saw was the portrait of Mrs. Kemp. It was probably the creepiest thing I had ever seen. Mrs. Kemp was wearing a red dress that was sparkly like it had a million sequins on it. She was wearing a pearl necklace and earrings. Her dark hair was styled like Jackie Onassis and her green eyes looked down at the viewer. Mrs. Kemp was sitting in a chair with her hands on her lap. She was also wearing long white opera gloves. The creepy part though was Mrs. Kemp's expression. She was looking at us like she knew we were up to something, which made a shiver run up my spine. Vickie, Demona and I stared for a few minutes and then Mama ushered us into the living room.

The living room was quite a spectacle. Mr. Kemp had strung Christmas lights up inside the house and had about a million candles lit. His Christmas tree was stunning. All the ornaments were clear cut glass that made a rainbow of colors reflect back into the room, like a disco ball would. There were glass bowls filled with pine cones and a wreath above the fireplace.

"Pretty good for an A/C guy, right?"

"It's beautiful Mr. Kemp," Mama replied.

"Please call me George. I have to give the credit to Mrs. Kemp though since she is the one to pick out all these decorations."

At the mention of Mrs. Kemp, Vickie and I glanced at each other. Soon the doorbell rang and more neighbors arrived. I asked Mr. Kemp if he wanted me to take the ladies' purses and coats. He said yes, and then Vickie volunteered to help. We both wanted to look around the house as much as possible so we would know how to get to the garage. As luck would have it, Mr. Kemp's house had the same floor plan as ours, so we knew right where the master bedroom was where we put all the coats and purses. This was great because it was easy to figure out how to get to the garage too.

When we got back to the living room, Mr. Kemp was serving punch and had opened up the buffet line. There was turkey, ham, potatoes, salad, rolls, and a host of other things people from the neighborhood had brought. This was turning out to be quite a party. Of course, we kids were busy eating and talking about what we wanted for Christmas. Vickie and I were whispering about the finer points of our plan.

After everyone was stuffed and the conversation had reached a lull, Mrs. Campbell suggested that we sing Christmas carols. This was it. Vickie stood up and suggested, "Rebecca has a song she has been practicing and would like to sing!"

"Oh isn't that cute!" said Mrs. Campbell.

"Come on in the middle baby," said Daddy proudly.

Little Rebecca smiled broadly. She began,

"On the fwurst day of Cwissmas my twue wub gabe to me..."

Vickie snapped a picture. Perfect I thought, now the flash wouldn't be distracting. Rebecca continued and all the adults kind of surrounded her not noticing Vickie and I had shrunk to the back of the crowd. We rounded the corner and went through the door that led to the garage. I felt for the light switch. Vickie must have gotten nervous, because she quickly took four pictures in quick succession. We got back into the living room just as Rebecca sang about the eight maids a milking. Vickie took the last of the pictures and victory was ours. Our friend Demona was a little disappointed that she didn't get to be a distraction, but we promised her the first viewing of the pictures.

Right before it was time to leave, Mr. Kemp said he wanted to propose a toast.

"I want to toast all of you for being here tonight. I also want to thank you all for all the kindness and support you have given me since the death of my wife. I especially want to thank Mr. and Mrs. Agnew and their girls for being so honest with me about some of the rumors about what happened. I would like to clear some of those up right now. First, I did not beat Mrs. Kemp. The bruises you saw were caused by a condition Mrs. Kemp had called hemophilia. Second, Mrs. Kemp was sad but she was taking medication to help her. Third, I don't know why she did what she did, but I guess she just couldn't handle some of her problems. Anyway, thanks for being here and Merry Christmas!"

It was the saddest toast I ever heard. Mama, and some of the other ladies had to wipe their eyes, and the men kind of weakly said, "Cheers". Everyone clinked their glasses, and then it was time to go home. Vickie grinned at me devilishly and pointed to her camera. She and I went back to the master bedroom and collected the coats and purses for the ladies. I gave Mama her coat. I wondered if when Mama passed the portrait of Mrs. Kemp if the expression on the painting would change. I was too afraid to look.

As we all walked home there was an uncomfortable silence. Neighbors peeled off the group until finally we were saying good night to the Campbells. Mama instructed Vickie, Rebecca, and I to go straight to bed. We got into our pajamas and into bed. Mama and Daddy came in for prayers and Daddy turned out the light when they left. Vickie and I began whispering about everything that had happened. We were so glad our plan had worked. We were going to have four pictures of where Mrs. Kemp hung herself, and we couldn't wait to see them. We decided to figure out how to get them developed in the morning, and then we both went to sleep.

Christmas Eve

I woke up later than usual the next morning. It was already 7:30am and I knew everyone else was up. I stumbled to the kitchen where Daddy was having coffee and reading the paper.

"Well good afternoon young lady."

"Morning Mama, morning Daddy."

"I guess staying out so late was tough on all of us," Daddy teased.

"Why are you still here, Daddy? Don't you have to go to work?"

"Have you forgotten that it is Christmas Eve? Besides I will go in for a little while to check on the dogs and what-not. You want to come?"

"Heck, yeah!"

Going to the shop where Daddy worked was fun. He worked in a scrap metal yard that my Aunt ran, and there were always treasures to be found. Once, Daddy brought home an old trumpet, and another time he brought home a whole collection of brass animals. He said someone had used them as decorations to go with and old Noah's Ark set. The animals were about two or three inches tall, and couldn't be scrapped, so Daddy brought them home.

Also, it was kind of fun to see the dogs they used as security at the shop. They were Dobermans and they had funny names. One of the dogs was named "Dammit" because when he was a little puppy, he was kind of bad and everyone at the shop used this word so much that the dog thought it was his name. The other dog's name was "Zacchaeus" after Daddy's favorite Bible story and song. I thought it was funny that one dog's name was a curse word and the other was from scripture. The dogs were the guards of the shop and they looked really mean and scary. I'll admit I was afraid of Dammit, but I knew Zacchaeus was a giant sweetheart that would rather lick you than bite. These two Dobermans were the replacement dogs that took over the shop after it burned to the ground. Two other German shepherd dogs Trouser and Sally were killed in the fire and for weeks Daddy was torn up about it.

"Go get dressed and you can go help me feed the dogs."

"Is a train coming in today?"

The trains came through to deliver more scrap metal from I don't know where. It was cool to see the trains come in with whatever was being delivered. Sometimes the trains brought smashed cars that were in little cubes. Sometimes the trains brought just piles of copper tubing, and occasionally the trains brought people hiding in the cars. Daddy always carried a little .38 with him when he opened the train cars. Once, a guy that had been on the train was lying under some papers and when Daddy opened the door, the guy punched Daddy in the face. Daddy pulled out the .38 and told the guy to leave. He left, and Daddy said he was sure that guy was going to kill him. I was glad Daddy had that gun too. I can't imagine Daddy ever really hurting someone, but you never know.

It is funny to think of my Daddy carrying around a gun all the time. Of course, back then it was just natural. Daddy had to deal with some sketchy characters at the shop sometimes, and they had even been robbed at gunpoint. There were big rats at the shop that were used for target practice (and pest control), and sometimes a rattlesnake was out in the yard. Daddy made sure to lock up the guns at home, except the .45 that was on top of the refrigerator and the other one in the headboard of Mama and Daddy's bed. We girls knew better than to ever touch those guns, because Daddy had given us a really vivid demonstration of what could happen if we did.

He took us out to the cotton field with about five or six watermelons. He took a marker and drew faces on the watermelons. Then he stood us a few feet away and shot two of the watermelons. Red pulp went everywhere, which Vickie and I thought was cool, but Daddy was serious.

"That represents your friends and your sister." Daddy said sternly. "They are dead now because someone who didn't know what they were doing used a gun."

Daddy then made Vickie and I shoot the other watermelons and then clean up the mess. Needless to say, we didn't touch those guns again unless Daddy took us shooting. Daddy had funny ways of teaching us girls sometimes, but they were effective. We always got the point, and respected Daddy enough to not question him. Mama didn't like some of his lessons though and worried that Daddy was raising tomboys.

After I was dressed and ready to go, Daddy and I made our way to the shop. First we stopped the little convenience store that was close to our house. We bought some doughnuts and a Big Red to snack on in the truck. Daddy's truck was old, and smelled of grease and oil, but it ran well and got us where we wanted to go. We got to the shop and Dammit and Zacchaeus greeted us noisily. They were hungry, and glad to have some human attention. We fed the dogs and then went out into the yard.

The yard was a wonderland of scrap metal. There were different piles for different metals, a furnace for melting down steel, a crane with a magnet attached, and it was dirty, and mysterious. Daddy let me go out on my own because the furnace wasn't lit, and he had the keys for the crane. I got to move the magnet on the crane once, which was like using a giant claw machine to pick up junk and move it to its correct pile. Daddy had gotten his arm broken once because he was holding a wrench and someone turned the powerful magnet on. It lifted Daddy off the ground and pinned his arm to the magnet.

I walked around a little while with Zacchaeus who was busy sniffing around for rats. I found a few things of interest, like some change someone had dropped, and a pin that looked like something my Grandma wore, but mostly just piles of junk. There was a train parked at the shop that had all the doors closed and locked so no one could get inside, but Daddy warned me to stay away from the train. Daddy was messing around with Dammit, giving him a chance to play fetch, and whatnot. We spent about an hour at the shop and then it was time to go.

"Hang on just a minute, Tonya."

Daddy went to the truck and took out a box. I knew what was inside.

"Merry Christmas, Zacchaeus. Merry Christmas, Dammit."

Daddy pulled out a large bone for each of the dogs. They barked and jumped excitedly and then took off with their bones. Daddy left the side door of the small office ajar, so the dogs could go there to sleep in the only heated area of the shop. My Aunt didn't like it when he did that, but Daddy wasn't about to let those dogs get cold. Also, he wanted them to have a way out of the shop in case it caught fire again. The dogs were there to protect the shop, and as far as I know, it was never robbed when they were there.

We got home at about 2:00 pm, because we stopped for a hamburger from the Whataburger. I loved their shakes and Daddy said since it was Christmas Eve I could have one. Mama was busy getting some of our Christmas dinner ready for the next day, and she was making pecan lady fingers for the Christmas party at my Aunt's house.

Every year, my Daddy's sisters had Christmas for their families on Christmas Eve. All my cousins and their children would go and there would be food and presents from my Aunts. My cousins were older than me, but their kids were right around me and Vickie's age. We would go down into the basement to play with each other until it was time to unwrap gifts. Mama didn't like going because she thought my Cousin's wives were a little snooty, but mostly I think Mama was jealous. My Daddy's sisters were all wealthy, and sometimes they forgot that we couldn't afford really nice gifts like they could. It was always a touchy situation.

Vickie and I loved going to our Aunts house because we liked to hear about where they had spent their vacations. My Aunts had been to Spain, and England which we thought was super cool. However, Vickie and I really loved to see what our Aunts had gotten us for Christmas, because despite being wealthy, our Aunts had the tackiest taste. For example, once I got a shirt that had the most awful picture of a clown on it. Vickie had gotten one with a weird ballerina on it. We laughed and laughed when we opened it, but we said our "Thank you" and then put them in the back of our closet.

Also, our Aunts had an unhealthy relationship with anything gold. Their house had more gold decorations than a gold shop. There were gold reindeer, gold Christmas trees, gold candles, gold furniture and even gold silverware. What wasn't gold was a deep red. Red couches, red chairs, red pillows, red tablecloths and red napkins were used. The whole place looked like a bordello. Mama said that wealth didn't mean taste, but I knew she was just jealous.

This year was going to prove to be a test for Mama though, because at some point, all the husbands of the family had gotten together and bought all their wives mink coats. When the time came for opening presents, all the men, except Daddy, left the room and brought back huge boxes. They counted to three and the women opened their beautiful new coats at once. They all squealed and put them on and squealed some more. There was poor Mama, with no fur coat to squeal about, and Daddy looking glum. Mama tried her best to be gracious and to compliment all the ladies, but it must have been really too much. Mama and Daddy didn't say a word the whole drive home.

Things brightened though when we got back to our neighborhood. We got back just in time for the Baby Jesus lighting. We all stood in the Crawford's driveway and Mrs. Crawford passed out candy canes and hot cocoa. There was a small fire built in a pit Daddy had made for the Crawfords. It was made from the bottom of one of the fifty gallon drums Daddy used at the shop to sort metal, and it had a stand too. Mr. Campbell was really excited about lighting Baby Jesus.

"Okay everyone. It's time to light our Lord and Savior. Ten, nine, eight, seven, six, five, four, three, two, one, Happy Birthday Jesus."

Baby Jesus lit up and we all cheered and hugged each other. I heard Mama say,

"This is better than that fur coat festival, for sure."

Daddy just smiled and hugged Mama. We drank our cocoa and then the Crawfords had to go to what they called Mass. I'd asked Mama about what it was and she said it was like our communion at church, only much more formal and mysterious. I asked if we could go sometime, but she said we would have to change religions.

It was time to go home and get ready for bed. There were no arguments or postponements on us kid's side, since Santa Clause wouldn't bring any gifts if we were still awake. We got in bed, and I reminded Daddy to put the fire out in the fireplace so Santa wouldn't burn his bottom. Daddy laughed and said he hadn't forgotten. We had cookies and Dr. Pepper out for Santa, because Daddy said he might like a break from all that milk, and we promptly tried our best to go to sleep fast.

I dreamed about the rabbit coat I had asked for from Santa. I dreamed that all my Aunts were mad because my rabbit coat was more beautiful and softer than their old stinky minks. In the dream, Mama just said,

"Well, sometimes people who deserve it get the better gifts."

Christmas

It was finally here. The day every kid in America dreams of and hopes for. The day when you got to see what Santa had brought you. The day when playing all day with your new toys and games was the only thing required. The day when you met your friends in the street to see what they had gotten from Santa. The day that was the most glorious of all. The day when your parents wished you slept late, but knew that was impossible. Their bleary eyes gleamed with the happiness they saw on the faces of their children.

I was awake before the sun. I had been instructed to stay in bed until Mama or Daddy came and got us kids, so we didn't accidentally see Santa before he had finished delivering our presents. My eyes just wouldn't stay closed no matter how hard I tried. Vickie was still buried under her covers though and I could hear Daddy snoring. I was so anxious to see what Santa had brought us. I was lying there thinking about all the gifts, and the stockings that Santa brought when Rebecca almost scared the bejesus out of me. She had crawled on the floor into me and Vickie's bedroom and tapped me on the arm.

"Is it Santa Claus time yet?"

"We have to wait for Mama and Daddy." I whispered.

Vickie poked her head out of the massive pile of covers she was under.

"Shhhh! It's not time yet!"

Rebecca was impatient. I motioned for her to crawl into my bed and we laid there for a while whispering about what Santa might have brought. Rebecca had asked for a Green Machine which was basically a souped up version of a big wheel. It was steered by two levers, and according to the commercial it could spin out too. It looked really cool. She had also asked for a Strawberry Shortcake bedspread. Strawberry Shortcake was her favorite character and Rebecca even said she wanted to be Strawberry Shortcake when she grew up.

I told Rebecca about the dream I'd had about the rabbit coat. I had also asked for a transistor radio that I could strap to the handle bars of my bicycle so I could listen to music while I rode to and from school. Vickie gave up on sleeping and joined the conversation. She had asked for a ten speed bicycle. She said her old bike was for little kids, but I thought it was neat. She said I could have it if Santa had brought her a new one. All of us knew there would be other surprise gifts from Santa and our stockings would be filled with apples, oranges, and nuts. This was what was always in our stockings.

Finally, I heard Mama and Daddy whispering. First Daddy went to the kitchen to get a pot of coffee going. Mama lay in bed for a while. Mama didn't like getting up in the mornings, so most of the time she laid in bed and twisted her hair. Once I asked her why she twisted her hair and she just said it was habit. Daddy said she was trying to twist out the ideas in her head.

When the coffee was ready and Daddy had poured Mama and himself a cup, they made their way to our room. They stopped at Rebecca's room first and when she wasn't there Daddy said,

"Maybe Santa Clause took her back to the North Pole with him."

"Daddy, I'm in here!" shouted Rebecca in my ear.

"Oh good! I thought you were going to have to shovel reindeer poo for Santa." Daddy joked and we all laughed.

"Well, I guess you all can go see what Santa brought."

All three of us raced to the living room. The Christmas tree lights were lit and because it was so early, it was the only light in the room. It was beautiful. We could see that there were presents piled in front of the tree, but what Santa had brought was laid out neatly into three piles. It was obvious Santa didn't want us to mix up our gifts and then fight over them. We all stood for a few moments just looking. Rebecca started jumping up and down pointing.

"A castle, a castle, a castle!"

It was a castle. It was a castle meant to be played with the Little People. Little People were like kids' action figures. The castle had a dungeon, a moat, and even some cannons. Rebecca loved it. She played with that castle for years.

"All right!" Vickie yelled.

She had her ten speed bicycle. It was silver and white with curled handle bars. She sat on it and read the instruction book about how to change the gears.

"Tonya, look over there," Mama said.

It was the most beautiful rabbit coat I had ever seen. It was made from all different colors of rabbits, and was patchwork looking. It had a zipper on the front and the collar would come up to your ears if the zipper was zipped the whole way. It was softer than a cloud, and was just the right length. It was a jacket that had black banding on the bottom and the cuffs to keep the cold wind from getting in. I put it on over my pajamas and Daddy took my picture. I had a huge smile on my face. As far as I was concerned, Christmas was complete. I couldn't wait to go back to school and show off in my new jacket.

We all sat down to begin the process of unwrapping the gifts. There were presents from my Aunts and Uncles, and Grandpa and Grandma. We opened those first. Uncle Randy had given us a sort of arcade shooting game. It was automated and everything. Uncle Gerald gave me a book and the Game of Life for me and Vickie to play. Grandpa and Grandma gave us sweaters. Then came the gifts from each other.

I gave Vickie a pocket knife I had found at the shop, and sharpened. I gave Rebecca a coloring book and a new box of eight crayons. I gave Mama some bubble bath. I gave Daddy some hunting socks, since they were the warmest kind. Everyone was pleased. Finally, Daddy was ready to give Mama his gift. This was a big deal because Daddy tried to really be nice to Mama on Christmas.

"Close your eyes, Honey, I will be right back."

Daddy went out the front door and we could hear some banging around in the garage. He knocked on the door, and when I opened it, Daddy had a huge box with a big bow on it loaded onto the wagon. I held the door open while he maneuvered it in.

"Okay, open your eyes."

"What in the world?" Mama's eyes widened.

"Well go on and open it."

Mama untied the bow and then sort of ripped open the side. She gasped and then finished opening the box. It was an automatic dishwasher! Mama began to cry.

"Well for pity's sake, honey, are you okay?" Daddy looked worried.

"I'm fine; it's just exactly what I wanted. Thank you honey, thank you."

Daddy looked relieved. Vickie and I were happy too, because now we wouldn't have to wash and dry the dishes. We just had to load and unload it.

Mama gave Daddy some new steel toed work boots which made Daddy very happy. Then we all just waited until breakfast was made and then we cleaned up the Christmas wrapping paper and relaxed for a while admiring our new gifts. I kept my rabbit coat on all morning and when I got dressed for the day, I put my coat on and wore it around the house.

When it was about noon, Grandpa, Grandma, Uncle Gerald, Uncle Randy, Aunt Linda, Aunt Vicki, and our cousins came over for Christmas dinner. We all thanked each other for the gifts we had gotten and then Vickie and I showed Marla and Gary the arcade game. We had a great time shooting the targets with marbles, and even Uncle Randy and Uncle Gerald took turns. We were having so much fun. Mama finally called us for dinner at about one.

All the adults sat at our big table, and we kids sat at the card table Daddy had set up in the living room. Vickie and Cousin Gary sat at our bar that looked into the kitchen, since they were too old for the kid table, and too young for the adult table. Mama brought out the ham for Daddy to slice for everyone.

Christmas dinner was always the same menu; ham, mashed potatoes, green beans, salad, rolls, cherry sauce for the ham, and for dessert pie. It was delicious and we all stuffed our faces. Grandpa was telling stories about the old days, and we kids were talking about the presents we had gotten. I was telling Cousin Marla about my new coat.

"EEeeeewwwww! Gross! You mean you are going to wear dead rabbits?"

"Well, just the skins I guess. I think it is beautiful."

"What's going on over there?" asked Mama.

"I was just telling Marla about my new coat," I answered.

Aunt Linda heard and said for me to go get it so she could see it.

"Can I?" I looked at Mama.

"Okay, but just for a minute, I don't want you to get food on it."

I went to my room, put on my coat, and just for good measure, brushed my hair. I strutted to the dining room with a huge smile on my face.

"Oh," said Aunt Linda. "I've never seen so many colors on one coat."

This didn't sound like a compliment. My smile faded.

"Feel how soft it is," I said.

"That's okay, I don't like to touch things like that," said Aunt Linda.

"Just what exactly are you saying Linda," Mama sounded upset.

"Nothing, Dolores, only that I don't like the idea of touching dead animals."

"I see." Mama was mad but she was holding it together.

By now I was feeling embarrassed and ashamed of my beautiful coat and I just wanted to die. Aunt Linda made a kind of phony smirk, and then Mama told me to take the coat back to my room and finish dinner. It was Grandpa who made things right.

"I bet that coat was the most expensive coat Santa's elves ever made. I mean, I suppose he had to pay each rabbit to sacrifice some of its fur for the coat. The way I see it, that coat has more love sewn into it than any other coat. You should feel very special that those rabbits sacrificed their fur for you."

I smiled and took my coat back to my room. After dinner, all the relatives left and it was time to just spend the rest of the day relaxing.

CHAPTER 12

Back to School

*T*he holidays were over and it was time to go back to school. We kids had grown tired of being at home with nothing to do, and so we were glad to be going back. I wasn't excited about seeing Mrs. Reed again, but I had a new book to read called "The Long Journey" so I was ready to have some free reading time. I was also looking forward to seeing Sean and showing him how pretty I was in my new coat. I was also looking forward to the standardized tests we would take because I always did well, and I thought it was kind of fun filling in all those bubbles.

It was cold outside so Mama was driving us to school on her way to work. The car line was kind of long so Mama dropped us off at the far corner of the school yard near the fifth grade hall. Vickie said I could go in that way if I didn't look like a dork. I tried to look grown up, but because I was short, some of the kids teased me and told me to go back to kindergarten. I just looked at them and went to my class. Sean was there and smiled when he saw me. I went over.

"Hey Sean, how was your Christmas?"

"It was great! I got to go hunting with my Dad and I shot a deer! Dad was really happy with me and we made deer jerky and had some venison for Christmas dinner. Also, I got a new pocketknife and a new hat. How was yours?"

"Mine was good too. I got this new coat, and a new book and some games."

"Hey, next time I go hunting maybe I can get a rabbit to make a hat to match your coat."

I loved Sean so much at that moment, I actually hugged him. He blushed and just said, "Golly".

"Sorry," I sputtered and went to my seat. My friend Janet made kissing faces at me and I was so embarrassed. I put my things away and waited for the bell. Sean sat next to me and kind of looked embarrassed too.

When the bell rang, Mrs. Reed led us in the Pledge of Allegiance and My Country Tis of Thee. Then she had some announcements before we started our math.

"Students, I hope you all had a very merry Christmas, and a nice break with your families. There are a few things you need to be aware of this morning. First, we are going to have a new student in our class who has just moved here from Dallas. His name is Bud Jenkins and he will be here shortly. He and his father have to take care of some papers in the front office so he will join us later. That also means that we are going to need to rearrange seats slightly to accommodate Bud. Sean, I am going to move you into the second group because they have only had three members and I would like Tonya to be Bud's class buddy to show him how things are run in the classroom. So Sean, will you please move and take your place tag with you so Bud will know right where to sit?"

Sean looked at me, and said "bye" and moved to another seat. Mrs. Reed was looking at me and I knew she did this on purpose and hated me. It seemed like Christmas hadn't made her any cheerier. She continued,

"Second, we will begin doing some practice drills to prepare you for the upcoming tests that the state requires. The tests have spelling, math, reading comprehension, and writing sections on them, so we will be focusing our attention on those subjects heavily in the next few weeks. I want you all to do well on the tests so you will be prepared for the fourth grade next year as well."

Just then Dr. Overby entered our class with the new kid and his Dad. Dr. Overby had been a basketball player in college, and he was very tall and kind of intimidating. The new kid was kind of big and he had a burr haircut. He was wearing a hunting jacket and had a pair of worn out boots on. He looked a little tough. Dr. Overby introduced him and then he and the new kid's dad left.

"Bud, my name is Mrs. Reed. This is our class."

"Hello," he said matter of factly.

"Class say hello to Bud."

"Hello, Bud," we all chimed. Bud kind of grinned.

"Bud, you will take the seat next to Tonya. She is going to be your class buddy for the next few days to help you learn where things are in the class and how the class is run."

"Okie dokey," said Bud, and I was surprised how casually he said it.

Bud sat down next to me and eyeballed me. He was trying to figure me out. When Mrs. Reed turned away to get the math books, Bud leaned over.

"You're kinda cute, and that coat is beautiful."

I was shocked and embarrassed. I had never had a boy compliment me like that, and I didn't know what to say. I glanced at Sean. Sean looked shocked and kinda mad.

"Thanks," was all I could get out.

When Mrs. Reed got the math books out, I told Bud where we were and how Mrs. Reed used her timer. He just looked blankly at the pages. I told Bud that we were just starting multiplication. Bud said okay and listened while Mrs. Reed gave her instructions for how to multiply numbers. When Mrs. Reed gave us the two pages in the workbook to do I started working. After a few minutes I noticed that Bud was still just staring at the pages.

"Do you need help or something?"

"Naw, I just don't feel like doing math. It's stupid and I ain't gonna do it."

"Don't you want a good grade?" I asked.

"I don't care about grades; all I care about is hunting. What good is math going to do me when I am out in the woods?"

I couldn't believe it. Bud made sense, but to outright defy doing work was beyond me.

"Hey, if you don't do your work, then I might get in trouble for not being a good class buddy."

"Yeah, okay, I'll do it for you since you are so cute and nice. I just hope you let me see some of your answers just to make sure I got them right. I bet you are smart too, right?"

"Well, I won't let you see my answers until you have the whole assignment done. That way it isn't cheating."

I was beginning to get annoyed with Bud's sweet talk and compliments. I figured he was just trying to manipulate me to get what he wanted. Bud reached over and patted my hand.

"Okay, I won't get you in trouble," Bud purred.

When the timer went off, we checked our answers and surprisingly, Bud got all of the problems right. I gave him back his paper but Bud didn't seem impressed. He just looked at me and smiled. I looked at Sean who looked sad. Sean didn't get a good grade and he knew he would be in trouble at home. Sean looked at me and I smiled. He smiled back.

"That your boyfriend?" Bud asked rather harshly. "Looks kinda wimpy. Does he cry when he gets bad grades?"

"Sean just wants to do well that's all. And no he's not my boyfriend; he is just a good friend."

"Oh, I see, well then he won't mind if I sit next to you at lunch then."

"We have assigned seats at the lunch table. Boys sit at one end and the girls sit at the other end."

Bud just shrugged and looked at Sean. Sean was looking at me questioningly and I didn't know what to do. Luckily, Mrs. Reed's timer went off and it was time for reading. Mrs. Reed was writing a children's book about two birds she called magpies, and so she was asking us to evaluate it by listening to her read it out loud. I didn't think it was very good because all the magpies did was steal things and then get in trouble. Also, none of us knew what a magpie was so it didn't make sense. We all moved our chairs to the reading rug and sat listening.

"Today, children our magpies steal firecrackers. Let's see what happens." Mrs. Reed was really excited about her book. I tried to look interested, but the drone of her voice was so dull I always got distracted.

I hadn't noticed that when we moved our chairs, Sean had sat on my left and Bud on my right. Sean had scooted his chair really close to mine and his arm was touching mine. Bud kind of slouched in his chair, but occasionally he would ask Mrs. Reed a question. This was unheard of, because Mrs. Reed didn't like her students talking. Finally, Bud asked the question everyone wanted to but was too afraid to ask.

"Mrs. Reed, if this is reading time shouldn't we be doing the reading and you the listening?"

Mrs. Reed put down her manuscript. She didn't look happy, but she scanned each of our faces.

"I suppose you are right Bud. Here is what we will do. Every other day I will read to you and that way you get the practice of listening. So for now I think we better get ready for recess."

Mrs. Reed looked a little disappointed, but the rest of us were glad that we wouldn't have to listen to that dumb story every day now. Since it was cold outside, our recess was in the cafeteria. Mrs. Reed grabbed the jump rope and balls and we lined up. Bud stuck close to me and so did Sean. I was beginning to feel like a rag doll being pulled in all directions. When we got to the cafeteria, some of the boys were playing a modified game of basketball using one of the cafeteria trash cans. Sean and Bud made their way over, and I went for the jump rope group.

After recess, we went back to the classroom to get our music lesson from Mrs. Echols, and then it was time for lunch. Bud kept crowding me in the line and Sean was doing the same thing. After lunch, there was science, then history, and finally time to go home. Mrs. Reed called Bud and me to her desk.

"Tonya, you did an excellent job today getting Bud incorporated into our class. I would like for you to continue for the rest of this week, just to make sure Bud feels comfortable and learns the class routines. Can you do that?"

"Yes Ma'am" I replied reluctantly. Bud smiled.

"Alright, you go get your coat on so you can go home. Bud, you must remember to take this note home to your father. It is just to explain how the day went and how well you did."

The bell rang and I went outside to meet up with Vickie to begin our cold walk home. Sean was waiting for me at the door.

"Hey, Tonya, are you going to be warm enough walking?" Sean was so sweet.

"Yeah, my new coat is super warm."

"Well here is something that will keep you warm all the way home," said Bud behind me.

Unbelievably Bud leaned over and kissed me right on the cheek! Right in front of our whole class, and worse in front of Sean.

My cheeks felt hot and I was so mad I started to cry. I looked straight at Bud and then smacked him upside his head with my lunchbox. Stunned he backed away. Sean was looking at me with those big brown eyes like a puppy that was so sad. But worse still, Vickie came up.

"What the heck is going on?" she bellowed.

"Aw I just gave her a little kiss and she whacked me with her lunchbox." Bud answered.

"Hey, kid, I don't know who you are, but that's my sister and if she wants you to kiss her she will let you know. Otherwise you just leave her alone." Vickie grabbed my arm and hurried me away.

"Listen, boys are just stupid sometimes, but you can't just smack them when they do something you don't like.

You have to use your head and get out of the situation. Then you can smack them if you want. What if your teacher had seen you hit him? She would have called Mama and Daddy and then you would get it."

I was so glad to have a big sister just then. I began to think about a way to get back at Bud and put things right with Sean. Vickie saw me thinking.

"Hey, that kid that kissed you lives in that house down the street from us that was for sale. Maybe you should go apologize before we go home so you don't get in trouble."

"Oh jeeez! Do I have to?"

"Yes, dummy, or then his parents will call Mama and Daddy and then you could get in trouble for sure!"

"Okay, I will on the way home."

Just then a car pulled up. Bud's father rolled down the window.

"You girls live just down the street from us; do you want a ride home?"

"No sir, we don't know you well enough to get into the car so we will just walk."

"Suit yourself," was his reply and as he drove away Bud thumbed his nose at me.

Vickie saw and said that Bud was probably too embarrassed to say anything to his parents so I didn't have to worry about it. I was worried though. I was worried that Sean would think I had cheated on him in some way and wouldn't be my friend anymore. I decided to call him when I got home.

I went into Mama and Daddy's room to call Sean. They had a little phone on the nightstand and I shut the door for privacy. I dialed his number. Sean's mother answered but said I could talk to Sean for a minute.

"Sean, I am sorry about what happened after school. I don't like Bud or anything, and I didn't want him to kiss me for sure."

"That's okay; I know you don't like him. Tonya, will you be my girlfriend?"

"Oh yes Sean!" I was ecstatic. I didn't know what we were supposed to do next so I just said,

"I will see you tomorrow! I have to do homework."

"Okay, I will see you tomorrow, sweetie."

Sean hung up real fast and I did too. Then I lay back on Mama's bed and closed my eyes. I was thinking of how it would feel if Sean kissed my cheek. Vickie came in the room. She looked serious.

"Hey listen, you better tell Mama and Daddy what happened today. It will be better if they hear it from you rather than someone else."

I was dreading beyond belief having to tell Mama and Daddy that some boy had kissed me. I thought they might not be really mad about me smacking him with my lunchbox, but I wasn't sure. I felt like Daddy might want to smack Bud too, and that made me feel nervous too. This was a situation that I just couldn't win. I waited until after dinner, and asked Mama and Daddy to come to the living room. They looked at each other and sat down on the blue couch.

"Mama and Daddy, I did something bad today," I began. "A boy kissed me on the cheek today at school and I got mad and whacked him with my lunchbox."

Mama and Daddy looked at each other and burst out laughing. They both laughed for a long time and both started coughing. I just looked at them and then I got kinda mad.

"Hey, it isn't funny!" I yelled and ran to my bedroom. I threw myself on my bed and cried and cried. After a while Mama came in.

"I'm sorry we laughed, honey. We didn't mean to make you cry. We were just so relieved because both of us had gotten a call from Bud's father saying he needed to talk to us about something serious that had happened between you and Bud. They are coming over at seven to talk things out."

"Mama, am I going to get in trouble?"

"Well honey, you know better than to hit people, but the way I see it, you were defending yourself. We will see what Mr. Jenkins has to say about it when he and Bud get here."

The thought of having Bud in my house was disturbing. He would know where I live and could come over any time he wanted. Mama told me to wash my face and brush my teeth. I waited for Bud and his Daddy in my room trying to distract myself by reading my new book.

In the story, Laurie, the girl, had to ride her horse to another town to get a doctor for her Grandpa. She had some gold in a pouch around her neck and a bad man was trying to steal it from her. She had to run away several times, and even had to wait out a forest fire. The story was really getting good, and there was the ringing of the doorbell.

I got up, went to the living room, just in time to hear Daddy invite Bud and Mr. Jenkins into the house. He asked them to come to the family room since we had a warm fire going. Mr. Jenkins thanked Daddy. Mama waved me over, and I saw Bud. He looked at me and smiled, then looked at the ground.

"Mr. Agnew," Bud's Daddy started, "Bud here tells me that Tonya smacked him with a lunchbox today."

"Yes, Mr. Jenkins," Daddy replied. "I think we better let Tonya do her own talking."

I was scared to death. I didn't know what to say and I didn't want to get in trouble, so I just swallowed really hard and told the truth.

"Well, Bud kind of came up behind me and kissed me on the cheek. I was surprised and I just swung around and hit him with my lunchbox. I'm sorry."

Mr. Jenkins looked at Bud. Bud nodded and then he said he was sorry too. Mr. Jenkins seemed satisfied and thanked Mama and Daddy for talking this over. Daddy wasn't done though.

"Well Mr. Jenkins, I am glad Bud is sorry and all, but I think maybe he needs to help me down at the shop for a couple of Saturdays, so he can learn about being respectful to girls."

"All right, he will come this Saturday and next Saturday. It will do him good to do some work."

Mr. Jenkins and Bud left. I didn't know what to say. Daddy cleared things up right away though.

"Young lady, you will be joining Bud and me at the shop. I want you two to work together so you both learn your lesson."

I stared at Daddy for a long time silently wondering why he didn't love me anymore. Finally, he told me to go get my homework finished and get ready for bed.

After Vickie and I got in bed, she asked me about my punishment. We talked for a long time and came to the consensus that Daddy was doing this so he could see what kind of boy Bud was, and to punish me for hitting him. I could only imagine what "project" Daddy would have for us. Usually, when we had to work at the shop it was just moving one pile of junk to a new spot in the yard. But sometimes, Daddy was creative and would make us do something no one else wanted to do like clean the bathrooms or something. At any rate, I was going to have to spend two Saturdays with this numbskull.

CHAPTER 13

Crime and Punishment

Saturday morning came. I got up and dressed slowly, regretting I had been born. I had to spend an entire morning with that turkey, Bud. Daddy was waiting for me in the kitchen.

"You better get yourself a good breakfast. There is a lot to be done at the shop today." Daddy didn't exactly sound friendly this morning. I didn't think he was that mad, but I guess he was. Bud and his Daddy came to the house at about 7:30 and Daddy told Mr. Jenkins we would be home at about one o'clock. We all got in the truck with me sitting between Daddy and Bud. I scooted over real close to Daddy so my leg wouldn't touch Bud's. Bud was oddly quiet.

When we got to the corner where Mr. Kemps house, he was outside getting his morning paper. Daddy waved and Mr. Kemp waved back. I hadn't thought of Mr. Kemp since

Christmas. I wondered what his holiday was like being all alone with just the portrait of Mrs. Kemp to keep him company. Bud saw me looking and asked,

"Who's that?"

"That's Mr. Kemp."

"Oh, my Dad was talking to him the other day since he lives right across from us."

I thought about this for a while and decided to tell Bud about Mrs. Kemp when we were at the shop working and Daddy wasn't around.

Daddy didn't say much as we drove to the shop. I wondered why, because usually he was pretty talkative to people. He seemed to have something on his mind. As we drove, Bud occasionally asked a question about the shop. I told him all about the furnace, the crane, and of course about Dammit and Zacchaeus. Bud seemed a little surprised about me cursing in front of Daddy, but I explained that it was the dog's name and I couldn't help it.

When we pulled up in front of the shop, Daddy got out and opened the gate. Dammit and Zacchaeus ran to him to greet him.

"Dang, those are big dogs!" said Bud.

"Yeah, but they are friendly to most people. When you get out they will probably bark at you, so just call their names and tell them to come and they will know you are all right. Also, since me and Daddy are here, they probably will just sniff you."

"Alright," Bud said apprehensively.

Bud had a right to be a little scared. Dammit and Zacchaeus were Dobermans so they looked pretty intimidating. I got out of the truck and walked over to the dogs. Bud got out of the truck. Both dogs kind of looked at him and made their way over to sniff Bud. Bud stood really still and called the dogs just like I told him. Dammit came first and sniffed Bud and then licked his hand. Zacchaeus was too interested in me to pay Bud any attention.

"Y'all come on inside," Daddy told us.

"Okay for your work today, you two are going to learn how to sort metal into those barrels over there."

Daddy started by showing us aluminum, copper, and steel. He said there were different types of each, but for now we would just sort according to the general types. Daddy took us over to the pile of scrap metal we had to sort. It was huge! The pile was taller than Daddy and about eight feet across. I knew this was going to take forever, but I guess that was the point. Daddy got me and Bud some gloves so our hands wouldn't get cut, and we began sorting. The good thing about sorting metal is that sometimes you find something that is kind of cool like pocketknives, or military medals. The bad thing is, you are standing in the shop where it gets cold and drafty making your nose run. Soon we were both sniffing pretty hard. We both got into a groove pitching things into their proper container and soon Bud didn't need me to tell him which kind of metal was what. So of course we began talking.

"Hey, Bud? You moved from Dallas, right?"

"Yeah. My Mom and Dad worked at the newspaper there."

"No way! My Mom works at our newspaper here in town."

"I know. My Mom and your Mom used to go to school together and played tennis. She said she couldn't wait to get back in town to visit with her. That's how come my Mom and Dad got jobs at the same newspaper as your Mom."

"Hold on, is your Mom's name, Kay?"

"Yep." Bud replied.

"Mama said that they played really good as a pairs team in high school. How come I haven't seen your Mom yet?"

Bud looked down at his feet.

"Well, my Mom and Dad are getting a divorce," he kind of half whispered. He looked so sad for a minute that I forgot about the whole kissing incident.

"Oh, I'm sorry," I said.

"It's okay; I'm going to live with my Mom on weekends and with Dad during the week. That's so I can go to school at only one school at a time. It's all worked out, but I miss seeing my Mom every day."

I thought for a moment about how I would feel if I only got to see Mama two days out of the week. Then I thought about the fact that Bud and I were here at the shop working off our punishment on one of the days Bud got to see his Mama. I felt awful!

"Hey Bud?"

"Yeah."

"I think maybe I can get Daddy to let us quit doing this and have him show us how to operate the big magnet crane outside if you want."

I figured adding some kind of fun might make up for Bud missing his Mama. I was really turning into a girl.

"Neat!"

I told Bud to wait for me and continue working and went to find Daddy. Daddy was in the office making coffee for himself and hot cocoa for me and Bud. The office had two small rooms with a window that slid open for people to come get money for the scrap metal they sold the shop. It had a large truck scale out one side that allowed people with big loads to weigh their truck coming in full and leaving empty. That way my Aunt June could pay them based upon weight rather than by the piece. Daddy looked up from his stirring.

"Where's Bud? I was just going to come get y'all to warm up with some hot cocoa."

"Oh, he's still out at the scrap pile working. I was wondering if maybe we could stop sorting and work the crane."

I related to Daddy my and Bud's conversation and Daddy listened really quietly.

"You sure are a sweet girl," was all Daddy said.

Daddy yelled for Bud to come in and we drank our cocoa and Bud asked Daddy about a million questions about the shop, the scale and all the scrap metal. Finally, Daddy took us out into the yard and we hopped up into the cab of the crane. Bud's eyes lit up like candles when Daddy picked up a huge pile of metal and moved it from one pile to another. I have to admit, it was really cool to see. Daddy let Bud move a few piles around and then let me have a turn. After about an hour, Daddy said it was time to go home. All the way home, Bud talked and talked about everything at the shop. When we dropped him off, Bud's Mama was waiting for him. I got introduced and then Daddy said it was time for us to clean up. As we drove away, I turned in time to see Bud hug his Mama really hard. It was really sad.

CHAPTER 14

Love and Other Horrors

The next Monday, I was anxious about school for two reasons. First, it was the first official week of me and Sean being boyfriend and girlfriend, and second, I had to explain to Sean why I was going to be nice to Bud. I was so unsure about how to act, I forgot to get Rebecca's clothes ready for her. She came to the breakfast table wearing her brown pants and a purple shirt with her Sunday shoes on. She was so proud of her choices she cried and fussed when I told her she didn't match, and her shoes were only for Sunday. Her argument was that she was going to a church for preschool so that counted as a good reason to wear her Sunday shoes. She also thought that purple went with everything so she matched. After I employed the "Strawberry Shortcake" argument, she agreed to change. Rebecca loved two things in the world. The color purple, and Strawberry Shortcake. You could bribe her to do any-thing if you threw in one of those things in the deal.

"Rebecca, you know Strawberry Shortcake only wears pink, red and brown because those are colors of strawber-ries. So maybe if you put on your red shirt and your pink shoes you would look just like her."

Rebecca smiled and ran back to her room to change. When she returned she felt so proud of herself. She had done exactly as I said except her shirt was on backwards and her shoes were on the wrong feet. While I fixed her up, Mama served breakfast.

It was still cold outside so Mama made sure we got a hot breakfast. Today we were having waffles made with her old fashioned waffle iron. It was huge and bulky, but you could change the settings to make the waffles browner or lighter however you liked them. I liked mine really dark so Mama always made mine last. She was just getting the orange juice and milk poured when Daddy and Vickie showed up.

"Well, this looks like a good breakfast," said Daddy. "We need some peanut butter for them I think. You know, 'Man cannot live on bread alone, he must have peanut butter.'

This was one of Daddy's favorite quotes but Mama just rolled her eyes and got it. Mama wasn't exactly a morning person so sometimes she could be grumpy. I was preoccu-pied with Rebecca's clothes, but Vickie brought me back to reality.

"Hey Daddy? Can you take me to Kmart on Saturday? The pictures I took at Mr. Kemps Christmas party are supposed to be ready that day and I have some money to pay for them."

Of course Vickie neglected to say the money was really mine, but I was too excited thinking about the photos.

"Sure, but it will have to be in the afternoon because Bud and Tonya still owe me a Saturday of work at the shop."

"Okay, the claim ticket says after 3:00pm anyway so that's great."

Vickie gave me a slight kick under the table. She knew I was just as excited to see what we had captured in the garage. I was excited, but also a little scared. It would be neat to see a ghost on film, but then what?

Once breakfast was finished and the dishes cleared it was time for everyone to clear out for work or school. Vickie and I met up with our friends for the cold walk to school. We saw Bud and his Dad drive by and I thought about how the day would turn out. Vickie told Cheri, Tonda, Demona and Darren about the pictures and it was planned that we would all meet in our backyard to review the photos together. We were discussing this as we passed Mr. Kemp's house. We didn't cross to the other side of the street like we used to because we had all been in the house and therefore weren't scared anymore. However, none of us could bring ourselves to look into the garage even though the garage door was opened. Mr. Kemp was pulling his car out to let it warm up before he went to work. He waved at us, and we all waved back.

By the time we got to school, I was so nervous I think my teeth were chattering and not because of the cold. Vickie left me at the corner to go into the 5th grade hall and me and the others went to the 3rd and 4th grade hall. I went to Mrs. Reed's classroom and put my coat away. Mrs. Reed was at the board putting up some warm up math problems on the board. I sat down at my desk and got all my supplies out. Neither Sean nor Bud was there yet, but I figured they were still outside playing kickball.

Mrs. Reed saw me and said,

"Now Tonya, don't start on these math problems until the final tardy bell has rung and I have started the timer. It wouldn't be fair if you got a head start."

I had no intention of doing math earlier than necessary, because even though I was pretty good at it, I didn't like it. My friend Janet came in and we talked about the Wild Kingdom episode that was on Sunday. Janet loved animals as much as I did, and so we often talked about horses and cows and stuff like that. Janet had her own horse and was learning English riding. I thought the outfit was cute, but I couldn't see the point of jumping over stuff without needing to. The horses I rode were at my cousin's ranch and they were working cattle horses. They only jumped at the cows to get them moving in the right direction, or to cut one from the herd.

Finally, the first bell rang and all my classmates started coming in. Sean came in and looked at me shyly and smiled. I felt my face get hot and I smiled back. Janet saw and she started giggling. I shot her a hard look and then giggled too. Soon, Bud came in and kind of plonked into his seat next to me.

He looked at me and said, "Well hey there scrap metal partner!"

Sean looked at me suspiciously, so I knew I had some explaining to do. I looked at Bud who was watching Sean and me and just said, "Hey."

The second tardy bell rang and Mrs. Reed began by saying that we would stand and say the Pledge of Allegiance and then begin our math warm up problems. We said the Pledge and Mrs. Reed began timing. Of course, I finished fast because I had done the problems in my head while waiting for everyone else. I pulled out "Charlotte's Web" and began reading. Bud leaned over and whispered,

"If I saw a spider that big, I would squish it for you."

Bud couldn't have known about my attachment to Charlotte. I looked at him sternly and said,

"If I ever see you squish anything, you better believe I'd squish you!"

Bud cracked up laughing. Mrs. Reed looked up from her desk.

"Bud, would you like to tell the class what is so funny?"

"Well, yes Mrs. Reed I would. Tonya said she would squish me if I squished any bugs for her."

The whole class erupted. I guess they were picturing little me, squishing bulky Bud. Mrs. Reed though was less than amused.

"Tonya, we do not condone violence in this classroom. Apologize to Bud for that remark."

"I'm sorry Bud," was all I could squeak out. I was so embarrassed.

Mrs. Reed was getting flustered already. She shushed us all and resumed timing the warm up problems. I could tell this was going to be a tough day.

Later, at recess time, Sean came over to the jump rope group and asked me if he could talk to me. After much "oooing and aaaahhhing" I followed Sean to one of the tables.

"So, girlfriend, how was your weekend?" Sean must have practiced what to say. I beamed.

"It was good except I had to spend some time at my Daddy's shop working with Bud. That was my punishment for hitting him with my lunchbox." I wondered if this was the right time for me to tell Sean about Bud's parents, but Sean let me know it wasn't.

"Well, that guy better watch out around you. You're my girlfriend and if he gets you in trouble with Mrs. Reed again, I'm gonna sock him in the eye!"

This was a new side of Sean I hadn't seen before. I liked it. I felt like he was the best boyfriend ever for wanting to protect me from Mrs. Reed. However, I didn't want Bud to get socked on account of his situation so I was torn.

"Well, I'm pretty good about keeping him in his place, but if I need your help, I'll ask for it, okay?"

Sean looked at me with those dreamy brown eyes and smiled so sweetly. I melted. Then I felt all weird, because I thought about kissing him which is what Bud had done to me. Love sure was confusing.

When we got back to the classroom, Mrs. Reed had an announcement.

"Class, as you know, Valentine's Day is coming up so I thought we should get to work on our Valentine boxes. I have obtained a shoebox for each of you to decorate as you wish. We have some nice pink, red, and white paper you can make hearts from, or if you wish to use paper doilies and paint, or yarn or just whatever you wish, you are free to decorate your box. On February 14th, we will have a small party and you are to bring Valentines for each person in the class. That way, everyone will get 20 Valentines that day from your classmates to show how much you care for each other."

"Mrs. Reed, you'll have a box too so we can give you Valentines too, right?" said stupid Darla.

"Well aren't you just the sweetest thing?" cooed Mrs. Reed.

I felt like throwing up. I looked at Sean and he put his finger in his mouth and made a gagging face. I giggled and so did Bud. I looked at Bud and was annoyed that he seemed to be watching everything Sean and I did.

"Well, yes I will make a box as well. Now let's get started. Please send only one person in the group to gather supplies for their table."

I was thrilled at this because this meant we didn't have to hear Mrs. Reed's weird magpie story. Also, I could have time to think about what I would write on all the Valentines. Of course I thought of Sean's first. I was thinking of writing, "From your girlfriend on Valentine's Day."

For my friend Janet, I would draw a horse for her and say something like "Giddy up". For stupid Darla I decided "To the teacher's pet". About that time, Bud leaned over to borrow my scissors. For his Valentine I would have to do some thinking. It had to be nice, but not too nice. I didn't want him to get the wrong idea. I finally decided on "From your neighbor". This seemed good because it was true, and not too mushy, just casual. Then I began to think about what Sean and Bud would write on my Valentines. I felt excited and weird at the same time.

After school that day, we all walked home and talked about Valentine's Day. Vickie had a lot to say because a lot of the fifth grade boys liked her. She was their best quarterback and could outrun everyone. The boys liked that. She liked playing the boys' games better because all the girls wanted to talk about was Sean Cassidy or his brother David. There was also a singer named David Essex, but once our Mama heard us talking about him and she got mad. We didn't know why, but she just said she didn't like his last name and little girls shouldn't talk about him.

When we got home, I finished my homework and began making my Valentines. Mrs. Reed had given out a list of everyone in the class so we could make enough Valentines, one for each person. There were 20 kids in my class, so I set out to work. I looked at the list and divided into kids I liked, kids I didn't like, and kids I didn't really play with. I decided to start with the kids I didn't really play with because they were easy. All you had to write was "Happy Valentines!" and sign your name. Next, came the kids I didn't like. I tended to personalize these with sort of sassy things like, "Hope you aren't heartbroken on Valentines". Or maybe, "Don't worry, Valentines is only one day a year." Once I started working on the kids I liked, it was fun, because you could draw pictures and say things that were your inside jokes. Last but not least, I made one for Mrs. Reed. Hers was tough because we weren't exactly on the best of terms. Finally I decided to draw a picture of me reading a book, her with her timer in her hand, and saying, "You have ten seconds to say Happy Valentine's Day." I thought it was kind of funny.

I folded and sealed each Valentine with tape and put them in a folder from school. I was excited in a way. Vickie had been working on her Valentines too and we both finished in time for dinner. Daddy came home and we sat down to eat.

"Well, girls, tomorrow is Valentine's Day!" said Daddy.

"Yep" was all we said.

I think Vickie and I were trying to ignore the topic because this was just one way for Daddy and Mama to tease us about boys. Still, Daddy wouldn't give up.

"Well, if y'all get too many Valentines from the boys, just let me know and I'll take care of it." Here, he paused for a second and added, "With a swift kick to the butt!"

"John! Don't curse in front of the kids," Mama exclaimed.

Daddy just laughed and Mama giggled too. Vickie looked at me and rolled her eyes. I did the same. After dinner, we watched an episode of Alfred Hitchcock and then got ready for bed.

I was thinking about all the Valentines I had done, and getting kind of nervous for no reason. Vickie turned over.

"Hey, do you think Daddy will get us boxes of chocolates like he usually does?"

"I guess," I replied.

"I hope so. I think this kid at school likes me. His name is Lane. He's kinda cute, but dang he can't catch a ball. I don't think I can like a boy who can't catch."

I didn't know why she was talking to me about it, but I couldn't resist teasing her about it.

"Vickie and Lane sittin in a tree,

K-I-S-S-I-N-G,

First comes love, then comes marriage,

Then comes Vickie with a baby carriage."

"Shut up you dummy!" was all she said, but I could see she was embarrassed.

I turned over and thought about my Valentines box, and all the nice things people would put on the Valentines. I couldn't wait.

The next morning at school, everyone brought their Valentines. Mrs. Reed decided that everyone would deliver their Valentines secretly. She decided that everyone would wait on the outside benches and she would allow two kids to come in and put their Valentines into the boxes. I don't know why she thought that would be secret, but she seemed really excited about this way of doing it. The first pair of kids to go was Bud and stupid Darla. After a few minutes, they came out and two more went in. Darla sat next to me on the bench.

"I know something you don't know," she sing songed.

"What, Darla?"

"I'm not telling. You'll find out." She giggled and traded places with Janet. I wanted to punch her.

Janet just looked at me and shrugged. Finally everyone had delivered their Valentines. Mrs. Reed looked pleased and said we could go in and get our boxes then return to our desk and look at our Valentines. When we went in, I noticed that my box looked fuller than the others. It was kind of heavy too. I took it to my desk and opened it. I wanted to die!

Bud had put a box of chocolates and 20 Valentines just for me in there! I looked at Bud and he said,

"I only gave Valentines to the one I love the most."

I didn't know what to say. It was sweet, and I knew about his Mama, and I felt sad for him, and I had a boyfriend, and I felt sorry for him, and Sean was dreamy, and oh my gosh Darla knows!

This last part horrified me most. I looked at her and she made this weird googly eyes and blew kisses. I looked at her and ground my fist into my hand. She raised her hand.

"Mrs. Reed, how come Tonya got more Valentines than anyone? Isn't that cheating?" Darla smirked at me.

"Tonya, can you bring your box here please?" said Mrs. Reed.

As I walked by Darla's desk I whispered, "You're going to get it!" Darla responded by tearing the Valentine I had made her in half. I was steaming.

Mrs. Reed looked at the contents of my box. She didn't seem to know what to say. Finally, she said to me quietly,

"Tonya, I think it's nice that Bud showed such appreciation for all the help you have given him. Don't worry about jealous girls, they aren't worth thinking about."

Did I hear correctly? Did Mrs. Reed just put down stupid Darla? I looked at Mrs. Reed not knowing what to say. Finally, I squeaked out, "Thanks."

"Go back to your seat now."

"Yes M'aam."

I walked back past Darla and she giggled, but I just turned up my nose and kept walking. Sean gave me a look. He held up the Valentine Darla had given him and ripped it in half. I smiled widely.

When I got back into my seat, Bud leaned over and whispered.

"I just wrote the word FART on Darla's Valentine."

I giggled and Bud smiled.

CHAPTER 15

Field Day

It was the best time of year. Spring had come which meant our time in school was interrupted by two things: tornado drills and Field Day. Tornado drills were kind of fun, because when the horn sounded, there were always a few people who screamed which made the teachers mad, and also, you got to go in the hallway and cover your head with your hands and sit cross legged. Some of the girls would cry. I thought they were babies. One time it was really stormy outside and the alarm sounded, so a lot of kids thought it was for real. My sister, Vickie, left her class hallway and found me to sit next to me. I don't know if she was scared or just protecting me, but I think it was a little of both. She didn't even get into trouble though because she lied and said she had been in the bathroom when the alarm sounded. Even Mrs. Reed didn't get mad. I think she was afraid of Vickie.

Field Day was something altogether exciting. I loved it! It was a chance to show how good you were at running, kicking, playing flag football, baseball, and jump rope and doing gymnastic stunts on the playground. Neither Vickie nor I had had any lessons in tumbling, but we were both really good at handstands. We practiced all the time in our front yard and had contests to see who could hold it the longest. We also ran races in the street with the other kids. We played catch with a baseball and would see who could throw it the hardest. Mama was worried about her tomboy girls, but we just had fun. Lately, we had been practicing our Frisbee skills since we were going camping with Cheri's family and we wanted to show off. We could catch it between our legs, behind our backs, and could bounce it off our fingers.

Field Day was really about a week long with each day featuring a few different events. It was like the Olympics and we were all excited to win ribbons. I had my eye on the tumbling and gymnastics events. I wanted to be an Olympic gymnast but that was an impossible dream. However, Field Day was a reality I could achieve. I did have some stiff competition from a girl named Kayla. She was really good and had trained in a real gym, so I was nervous. However, Kayla was also really nice and I thought if I beat her, she wouldn't talk to me anymore. I didn't want that, but still wanted to win. Such are the conflicts of youth.

The night before Field Day Vickie and I whispered back and forth about the upcoming week.

"Hey, are you going to do the flag football competition?" I asked.

"Heck yeah! I have to since I'm the quarterback. I learned a new play we have been practicing called the quarterback sneak. I can't wait to see the other team's faces when we pull it off and I get to score." Vickie was really excited.

"Neat! What do you do?"

"Well, you know when I hike the ball? Well, instead of handing it off or passing, I pretend to hand it off and then while the other team is watching the running back, I sneak passed their defensive line and score. It all depends on the running back being a good pretender, and the element of surprise. It's going to be super cool!"

I didn't know much about football, since Daddy and I watched baseball mostly. However, I thought Vickie was being smart putting together a strategy.

"Hey, do you think I can win the handspring contest?"

"How many can you do in a row?"

"I think I can do four, but if I get it right I can do five."

"Back or front?"

"Front. I'm too scared to do back ones. Throwing your head at the ground backwards is scary."

"You probably can get a medal. I know you can win the handstand contest though. You are up to two minutes!"

"Yeah, if they don't count on my arms shaking, I can do it."

"No, dummy, all you have to do is outlast the others. Of course if you want to set a record then that is different."

"Yep, definitely going to set a record. That's what I want in the worst way."

"Well, good luck. We better be quiet."

I laid there dreaming of winning a medal and setting a record for the longest handstand. I saw myself with leaves on my head and a big shiny gold medal on a ribbon around my neck. It was going to be neato torpedo!

The next day, our class was so stirred up by the possibilities of Field Day we couldn't focus on our math warm ups. I even missed one, which was a rarity. Mrs. Reed was upset.

"Class, if the behavior in this room doesn't improve, we will not participate in today's Field Day events."

We all knew this wasn't an empty threat so we got really quiet. Darla raised her hand.

"Mrs. Reed? If we aren't going to participate in Field Day, what do we do?"

I knew that Darla was talking about herself, because she was just about the most worthless girl on the field as possible. She would shriek if a ball came near her, cry if she got her dress dirty, pout if her hair got messed up, and throw a tantrum when she was always picked last. What did she expect? Did she think the team captains were thinking, "Oh, we want the worst player on our team because we don't want to win?" Also, it didn't help that me and a girl named Sherry were always captains of the girls' teams and Sherry couldn't stand Darla either.

"Well, Darla, you should cheer on the other competitors as a show of good will," said Mrs. Reed.

"Can I do some cheers I learned from my sister who is a cheerleader in high school?"

"Yes, Darla, that will be fine."

Everyone could tell Mrs. Reed was just trying to shut her up, but Darla thought she had gained some respect mentioning her sister. Little did she know, that everyone thought her sister was also stupid.

We got back to our regular schedule of math, reading, and of course listening to a chapter from Mrs. Reed's magpie book. Finally lunch came, and the cafeteria was in an uproar. Field day would start just after lunch. I tried to not eat so much, so when I was doing my handstand I wouldn't throw up. Sean was sitting down the table from me and gave me thumbs up. I was so happy! Now I knew I would win. Just as we were leaving the cafeteria, the fifth graders came in. Vickie passed me and said,

"You better do good!"

I knew she didn't want people to make fun of her because of me, so I felt a new pressure. I couldn't let the family down. Her football game was later in the week, so I had better do good.

We lined up and filed outside. All the teachers of the third grade lined us up and finally our principal Dr. Overby announced,

"Let the games begin!"

First up were the parallel bars. This was a boy's only competition. They had to swing into a handstand and hold it. I wanted to try, but for some reason girls weren't allowed to do it. I guess they thought swinging your legs was not ladylike. I didn't pay much attention to the competition because next up was the handstand event for girls. My friend Janet suggested I do a couple to warm up. I thought that was a good idea so I just stayed up long enough to feel steady and then came down. Also, I didn't want anyone to know how long I could hold up before the real competition began. I was worried.

Finally, Dr. Overby announced that it was time for the handstand competition and all the girls participating should line up. Me and Janet stood next to each other on the line. Kayla was about three or four girls down from me. I took a deep breath.

"Okay girls, ready, set, go!"

I couldn't hear the crowd cheering or anything. I couldn't see the other girls competing. I could only hear the blood in my ears and after what seemed like an eternity, my arms began to shake. I took another deep breath and held that handstand as though my life depended on it. I heard the whistle and knew the contest was over and there was a winner. Then I realized that it was me! I kept going though because the timer was still counting. I never worked so hard. I thought at one point that I was coming down, but instead I just took a little baby step on my hands. The crowd went crazy. Finally, I had to come down or else fall down. I put down my legs and stood up a little dizzy from the blood leaving my head. For some reason I was breathless. Janet was jumping up and down, Kayla was smiling, and the only person who wasn't cheering was Darla. Who cared?! I had won. My time was a ridiculous three minutes and fifteen seconds. I couldn't believe it!

"Wow!" screamed Janet. "That was amazing!"

"Great job, Tonya," said Kayla. I was so glad she was still talking to me. She added, "You should join my gymnastics class. You would be so good at it."

I was floored. Not only was she a good sport, she wanted me to get better too. That's what's called real sportsmanship.

I caught my breath and Dr. Overby came over with my medal. I was so proud. He gave me five and went on to the next competition.

Sean came over and kind of patted my back. He was so proud of me and I was thrilled. Bud looked at me and winked which made me feel weird. Darla scowled and fluffed up her hair. I loved that she was jealous of little old me.

After the handstand event, the boys competed in the 100 yard dash. Sean won that and another kid named Jeffrey came in second. Next it was the girls turn to compete. I was entered into this contest too along with Janet, Sherry, Kayla and other girls from other classes. I was feeling so good, I hoped to do well. I think there were about ten girls, but I knew one girl named Patty wouldn't be hard to beat. She had a nickname that wasn't very nice. It was Fatty Patty. I felt sorry for her because even though she was big, she still competed and that took guts. Also, she could draw better than just about anyone I ever knew.

Dr. Overby got us lined up.

"Okay girls, on your mark, get set, go!"

I ran like the devil himself was chasing me, but I could see Kayla getting ahead. Sherry also got ahead of me and we ended the race in first, second, and third respectively. I was glad Kayla won. I congratulated her just as she had me. Janet finished in fourth and poor Patty finished last. I told her "good job" anyway just to be nice.

After the race, it was time for the boys to compete throwing a football through a tire. They had to see how many they could get in a row. I couldn't have been less interested since none of the boys from my class competed. This one kid named Gino got the most. He was a really big kid and later, he played professional football. I guess Field Day was just a stepping stone for him.

Next was the handspring contest. I was only doing the front ones. There were six girls competing and of course Kayla was one of them. Another girl named Andrea who also took gymnastic classes was our biggest competition. We all got ready for the first girl, but she only did two and bounced out. She was mad. Next came poor Patty, who tried her best, but could only do one. I didn't want to go next to show her up, but it was my turn. I took a breath, then took my running start and got five in a row! I was happy because that was my personal best.

Dr. Overby shouted, "Now we have a contest!"

Kayla did her turn and tied with me. That made me feel good. Next came Andrea. She took her running steps and

I could tell I was in trouble. She had really strong looking legs. To everyone's surprise Andrea threw eight handsprings in a row! We were all beside ourselves with glee. We jumped up and down and gave her fives. I felt sorry for the last girl because she didn't stand a chance. She was a new girl to our school and just entered the competition so she could try to fit in. Her name was Lia. She did pretty good though and did four in a row which was respectable considering what Andrea had just done.

So my Field Day competitions were all done. I had a gold medal, a silver medal and a bronze medal. I could tell my Olympic Days were yet to come. I watched the boys do a kick ball game and the girls do their back handsprings. I had wished I could do it, but I was just too afraid. Kayla won that one doing a shocking six back handsprings in a row. I think she could have done one more but she pulled out at the last second. That happens sometimes. Your body just kind of says "Nope!" and no matter what you do, you can't control it. Day one of Field Day was complete. We headed back to class out of breath but happy.

"Now, class, I know you are tired, but we must practice for our State Exams that are coming up. Today, we will practice some reading comprehension exercises," said Mrs. Reed.

I was glad about that, because I was good at reading and could comprehend with the best of them. Basically, you just had to read a paragraph and answer some questions. Some of the questions seemed tricky at first, but if you read the question slowly, then the answer was easier. Also, sometimes it seemed like the questions were meant to trick you, so I would think about what I would do if I was going to write a trick question. Once I figured that out, then all those tests became easier. I was tired after the Field Day events so I got one of the questions wrong. It made me mad because I wanted to get 100% on the state test.

The day ended and we started on our way home. Vickie was in a great mood because she had heard about my winnings. She was talking to everybody else about the upcoming football game and got caught up discussing a new play with one of her team mates. She was determined to win. We got to our street and everyone started peeling off to their houses and finally it was just she and I walking the two or three houses to home. She was deep in thought but finally she said,

"Hey, this Saturday we get the pictures!"

I had almost forgotten about them, because Daddy had me and Bud working at the shop and for some reason or another a few Saturdays had passed and we still hadn't picked them up. Also, working at the shop with Daddy and Bud had become a regular thing and Bud was getting good at sorting. I didn't realize it too much but Bud and I had become friends although Bud was a little more interested in me than I in him.

"Oh yeah! Wow, I wonder if we caught a ghost on the film?"

"I don't know, but I can't wait to see.

CHAPTER 16

Revelations

It was the last Saturday that Bud and I had to work together. I was glad because the weather was starting to get nice and I wanted to spend time outside instead of the drafty warehouse sorting metal. Dammit and Zacchaeus had grown to like Bud because he always brought them some kind of bone. They didn't even bark at him anymore but instead wiggled from head to the tip of their short tails. They practically turned inside out when they greeted him. Bud really liked those dogs. Daddy and I picked Bud up on the way to the shop.

"Well good morning, Bud!"

"Hey there, Mr. Agnew."

"So this is the last Saturday we will be working together at the shop. So I thought we would take you to the Pancake House for breakfast first," said Daddy.

I wasn't too thrilled about that because that was me and Daddy's thing, and now I had to share it with Bud. But, I didn't mind too much because after all it was just one Saturday.

Bud seemed kind of excited about it, and I noticed that Bud seemed kind of excited about just about everything. He certainly had a lot of energy.

We pulled in and of course we were seated in Miss Mary's section. She poured Daddy some coffee and Bud and I some apple juice. I didn't order coffee this morning, because Bud might think I was acting too grown up. Since when did I start caring about what he thought of me? I don't know, but I just did. Miss Mary was intrigued by this boy.

"Well, now young man, are you Tonya's cousin or something?"

"No ma'am, I'm just a friend."

"Uh oh, that sounds serious, do I hear wedding bells?" Miss Mary and Daddy giggled.

I felt my face go hot and that just made Daddy and Miss Mary laugh harder. Bud nudged me with his foot and when I looked at him, he just smiled. I felt so weird! Finally, Miss Mary took our order and went to put it in.

"Mr. Agnew? Can I come to your shop sometimes this summer when school is out? I really like it there and I'm sure my Dad would let me."

"Sure, Bud. We will get it all arranged when I take you home this afternoon," Daddy replied.

"Hey Daddy, can I go with you to pick up the pictures today with you and Vickie?"

"Sure,"

Bud looked at me curiously.

"It's just some pictures Vickie took at the Christmas Party at Mr. Kemp's house," I explained.

"Oh, cool."

I hadn't told Bud the whole story, so I determined to do that today and then when we got the pictures, he could see for himself.

When we got to the shop and the dogs were greeted and fed, we set to work. There was a train in the yard this morning, so Daddy told me and Bud to stay in the shop while he checked the cars. Bud looked impressed when Daddy strapped on his pistol. I explained why he needed it. Bud nodded his head. After Daddy went out, I began telling Bud about Mr. and Mrs. Kemp and the portrait, and about how we had managed to get pictures of the garage. Bud listened intently and when I was done he said,

"Dang, that was a good plan! I hope y'all caught a ghost in the pictures."

"Yeah, me and Vickie came up with it, and it really worked out. It was really creepy being in that garage."

"Well, yeah, I mean the lady died in there!"

About that time, Daddy came back in the shop. He looked upset.

"Okay, so there has been a change of plans. I have to call the police and Bud I'm calling your Dad to come pick you up. Tonya, you have to stay in the office until I come get you. Is that clear?"

Daddy looked serious and it made me scared. Bud and I nodded and went straight to the office. Daddy called the police from the other room and I couldn't hear what he said. When he came back in, Daddy sat us down.

"Okay, so here's what the deal is. When I went to check the cars, the dogs alerted me to one of them. When I opened the door I found a guy who had been shot and he was dead. So I've called the police and when they get here they will want to talk to all three of us. Now don't be scared, they just want to find out our side of the story."

I almost fainted. Bud looked white. We both nodded and didn't say anything. I could tell Daddy was really upset because his jaw was set and his eyebrows were knitted almost into a knot. Daddy called Bud's daddy and then he called Mama and my Aunt June who owned the shop. Then we waited.

The police showed up with sirens blaring and a firetruck and ambulance came too. Pretty soon KLBK showed up with a reporter to get the story. They didn't talk to us, but they did talk to Daddy. Bud's daddy came and after the police had spoken to him they let him take Bud home. I had to stay until the police had taken a statement from Daddy and asked me a couple of questions. When they asked Daddy about his pistol, they understood and checked to see if any rounds had been fired. When they found none had, they let me and Daddy go home. Aunt June stayed to make sure the police had everything they needed and locked up the shop.

On the way home, Daddy was quiet. I knew he was upset so I didn't say anything. Finally, Daddy spoke.

"Honey, I don't want you to be afraid, okay?"

"Okay, Daddy."

"I don't want you to ever be afraid."

"I know, Daddy."

"Well, I think that's about all we need to say about this, okay?"

"Okay."

For the rest of the ride, Daddy was silent. I knew better than to ask him any questions. When we got home Mama gave him the longest hug I've ever seen her give. She hugged me real tight too and that made me cry a little. I don't know why I was crying, but I just was. Vickie looked at me really solemn and didn't ask any questions. Finally, we all went inside.

Later that afternoon, Vickie, Daddy and I went to Kmart. We went to the photo center and paid for the pictures. Vickie and I were excited to see what we captured so as soon as we got home we went straight to our room. The first few pictures were of little Rebecca singing and all the grown-ups watching. One of the pictures was kind of creepy because Mr. Kemp was looking straight at the camera and the portrait of Mrs. Kemp was over his shoulder. It was like they knew we were up to something. Finally, we got to the pictures of the garage. The first picture had

Vickie's finger in it, but we could make out Mr. Kemp's car. The next picture was a little blurry, but we could see the ceiling of the garage, and the cross beam across the middle. There was a blurry streak across the middle and Vickie and I both gasped! Was this a ghost? The last picture was clearer and there was no blurry streak across it. Vickie and I were convinced we had our ghost!

CHAPTER 17

Daddy's Little Einstein

The time had come for the state testing at school. I was a little nervous mostly because I wanted to do really well. I had my eye on getting a 100% on the Reading Comprehension. I didn't feel as confident about the Math section, but I felt pretty good about the Writing part. All our practices had been writing a story about something that had happened to us that was exciting, so I had plenty to write about. That morning, Mama made us bacon and eggs, toast, and orange juice for breakfast. She said it would make us smarter if we had a good breakfast. I couldn't stop thinking about if I had enough number two pencils and were they sharpened enough or too much. I also had a pink eraser I was worried would smudge my answer paper, or if I rubbed too hard would make a hole in it. If that happened, would they just stop grading my answers and make me go to summer school? That would be the worst! Only the really dumb kids went to summer school. Everyone knew that. I would have to move out of town if I had to go to summer school. I was lost in my thoughts when Vickie said,

"Hey, if I do really good on my tests today, they will let me try out early for the tennis team in junior high."

"Wow, that's great Vickie!" Mama said proudly.

Mama had been a champion tennis player in high school and she hoped one of us would be interested. She even gave tennis lessons one summer, but I didn't like it too much. Vickie, on the other hand, had taken to it just like any other sport she tried and was really good. So Vickie had more at stake with the testing than I did. That made me feel better. Little Rebecca wanted in on the conversation so she began chanting,

"One plus one is two, one plus two is three, and one plus three is four!"

"Very good, Rebecca!" Mama encouraged her.

"Well it looks like I'm surrounded by geniuses this morning," Daddy interjected. "You all will do just fine today so don't worry about it."

Daddy hadn't done well in school when he was younger because he said he didn't have good teachers, but later we learned that Daddy was slightly dyslexic so reading and writing was slow business for him. However, he was still able to keep a steady job and provide for his family, so the fact he wasn't a scholar didn't matter. He was however, one of the reasons I became a teacher.

We finished breakfast and got ready for school. We were headed down the street to meet whoever else was walking to school. We were all thinking about the tests we would take today when we passed the empty lot on 66th street. We stopped for a minute because whoever owned that lot had plowed and planted onions in it. We all stopped to see how the onions were doing. We knew that in a few weeks, we could stop by and pick one for a snack on the way home. Our moms hated when we did that because it made our breaths stink so bad. However, we thought it was cool to pick our own onion and eat it straight from the ground. We were weird kids.

When we finally got to school, there was a weird hush because everyone was thinking about the tests we were about to take. No one wanted to go to summer school, so the threat of not doing well was very real. Our family had planned to go on vacation with Cheri's family, so I didn't want to ruin that. Sean looked really nervous. I knew he was worried about the math section. I worried for him too. Bud came slouching in as usual, and patted me on the shoulder. I don't know why he did that, but in a weird way it made me feel more comfortable. We all sat down and when the bell rang we did the usual Pledge of Allegiance and My Country Tis of Thee. Then an announcement from Dr. Overby came over the loud speaker.

"Students, today you are taking the state testing exams. Your teachers have worked very hard to prepare you for these tests and want you to score well. I know you may be feeling nervous about the tests, but don't worry, you are prepared and you will do well. Do your best and good luck!"

I think he was trying to encourage us, but to me the announcement could have easily been translated in to kid language like this,

"Students, today you are determining your destiny. Your teachers will tell your parents not to love you anymore if you score badly, so watch it. You should be feeling nervous because this test is harder than anything you have ever done and will determine if you are a loser in life. Do your best, but just know that it won't be enough."

I looked at my friend Janet, who looked like she was going to puke. Sean tried to smile, but it just came out weak. Mrs. Reed was busy getting the answer sheets passed out and instructing us not to open them until it was time. At last, we were ready. Mrs. Reed explained that the tests were timed and we would have a certain amount of time to complete each section. Now I understood her obsession with her timer. She had been preparing us since day one. The first section was Math. We opened our tests and began.

After what seemed like half an eternity, the time was called. I almost cried. I hadn't finished the test! Some of the other kids moaned really loud. Mrs. Reed was less than sympathetic.

"Class, if you didn't finish this section in the allotted time, I suggest you pick up the pace for the next section. However, be as thorough as possible"

Sean looked at me and I could tell he hadn't finished either. Bud leaned over and whispered,

"Stupid test! I bet they knew no one would finish."

This made me feel better and lit a strange little fire inside me. I felt like I had been tricked by the testing people so boy was I going to show them! I bucked up and got ready to comprehend the heck out of the reading sections.

After all the testing for the morning was done, we had an early recess. I think Dr. Overby knew that having to sit for so long doing so much work was about to cause all the students to explode with energy. He gave us an extended free recess, which meant all the third grade classes were on the playground at one time. This was great because you could visit other friends in other classes. I got to join the jump rope group with my friend Tonda, and we visited with some of the other kids from the neighborhood. I told them that Vickie and I had the pictures back from the Christmas party and we set up a time to meet in the front yard to look at them. Everyone was very excited. At last, we all went in for lunch and then more testing. The day was very long. We knew this was the way school was going to be for the rest of the week, so we were all glad when the dismissal bell rang.

As we walked home, Vickie and the rest of us arranged to meet in our front yard after our afternoon snack to look at the pictures. Everyone was excitedly talking about what they would see, but Vickie and I weren't giving any clues. If we had charged admission, we would have made a bundle. When Vickie and I were having our snack, we talked about how to handle the pictures so everyone got to see them and how they should be narrated. We went outside to find about ten of our neighborhood friends waiting for us. Vickie said,

"Okay, everyone sit in a circle."

Everyone obeyed. The excitement was palpable.

My job was to hold the picture up first while Vickie explained what was happening in the picture and then I was to pass the picture to the person on the right. I was supposed to wait until the picture had made it around the circle before we went on to the next one. Solemnly, we began.

"In this first picture, you can see all the adults watching and listening to Little Rebecca sing her song. Notice, everyone is smiling except Mr. Kemp."

I hadn't noticed this fact, but sure enough it was true.

"Next we see the same scene, but now Mr. Kemp looks even gloomier."

This was true too. I didn't realize it at the time, but Vickie had a flair for the dramatic.

The next picture was the one of Mr. Kemp looking straight at the camera with the portrait of Mrs. Kemp in the background. It was super creepy.

"Here, Mr. Kemp is staring right at the camera and the picture of Mrs. Kemp is staring too. I'm not sure, but I think if you tilt the picture left and right, their eyes follow you."

Vickie was really getting into it now.

"Next, yes, that's my finger, but it is when we first opened the garage and I sort of just pointed and took the picture. You can see Mr. Kemp's car. Now before I show the next picture I want you to know that there was nothing wrong with my camera."

I held up the picture with the blurry streak. Our friends gasped.

"As you can see, there is a weird streak going across the place where the beam in the garage is. We believe that this is where Mrs. Kemp hung herself. So if you look closely you can kind of make out a rope with a face in it."

This last part was kind of exaggerated, but of course some of our friends saw it and some didn't.

"The last picture shows the exact same thing except this time there is no blurry streak. This proves that there was nothing wrong with my camera."

I passed around the last picture and then some kids wanted to compare them to each other. Remarkably, the angle, lighting, and exposure were exactly the same. The only difference was the blurry streak.

"I don't know," said a kid named Michael, "it kind of looks like you moved the camera in the middle of taking the picture."

"No, if you look," explained Vickie, "nothing else in the picture is blurry, and it would have been if I moved the camera."

"Maybe it's a bug," continued Michael, "it must've flown across the picture just at that second."

Vickie was beginning to get annoyed. I could see her eyes getting that steely look she got right before someone got a taste of a knuckle sandwich. However, she just kind of waved her hand away in a dismissive little flip. Some of the kids wanted to look at the pictures again so we passed them around again. Finally, we all voted that there was definitely a ghost in the picture and the matter was settled. We all started for our houses to get ready for dinner. Vickie and I went in and put the pictures in our top dresser drawer. But Vickie took the last picture and taped it to the mirror of the dresser so we could see it whenever we wanted. It was a creepy reminder of what had happened.

For the rest of the week, we were mired in the bogs of state testing, so we didn't really talk much about anything else at the dinner table. Of course, Mama and Daddy wanted to know all about it, so they asked about a million questions about how it was done and how we thought we did. I told Mama and Daddy about the first Math section and how I hadn't finished. Mama seemed worried, but Daddy had a different approach.

"Well, of the questions you did finish, do you think you got the answers right?"

"I'm pretty sure I did," I said thoughtfully.

"Then that's all that matters. If you answered them right, then who cares if you did it in record time?"

"Well," I said feeling better, "I think they want to see if you can answer correctly and fast."

Daddy didn't seem impressed.

"Well, that's just dumb. Why do you have to be fast about it? It's not like there is ever going to be a time in your life where someone runs up to you and says, 'Quick, solve this math problem or it's the end of the world!' so you just try to make sure the answer is right and don't worry about the timing."

Mama didn't feel the same way.

"Well, I think that having quick math skills can be useful too. Of course getting the right answer is important, but if you learn to do it quickly, then you won't waste the time in getting the answer."

I could see both sides of their argument, but the truth was that I felt like I had let myself down in not finishing. I finished dinner and doing the dishes and went to my room to go over some basic math facts. I had made myself some multiplication flash cards and was doing them when Vickie came in.

"Listen, those tests aren't really that important. I know you're thinking about summer school, but that's not going to happen. They only send the kids who don't do good on the test AND have bad grades. Since you have straight A's you don't have to worry about it."

I wanted to hug her for that, but I knew if I did she would be all weird about it, so I just nodded my head and started getting ready for bed.

CHAPTER 18

Alien Encounters

After two weeks of testing, all of us in Mrs. Reed's class were tired of school in general and we all had a hard time focusing on our work. Some of the boys got into trouble one morning, because they had put chalk in the spaces of the erasers Mrs. Reed used so when she tried to erase something on the board, there were these long chalk lines. We laughed, but Mrs. Reed scolded us for wasting chalk. I was getting restless too since I had finished reading "Charlotte's Web" again and the book I had gotten for Christmas for the second time. I was always looking for an excuse to go to the library to see if they had gotten any new books, but I had already read the ones that were on my level. The worst though, was having to listen to Mrs. Reed's stupid magpie story.

All of us in the class had gotten so tired of it when Mrs. Reed said it was time for listening, we moaned and groaned our way to reading circle. Poor Mrs. Reed didn't take the hint and would gleefully begin reading. Bud had adopted a slouching position on the chair and usually went to sleep. It was funny until one day he let out a little snore and got sent to the principal's office. He came back kind of half grinning though and later told us they let him go to the nurse's office to finish his nap.

Mrs. Reed had become increasingly excited about her book, because she had submitted it to a publisher and had received word back that they were editing it for publication. We didn't know what that meant, but we did know that we were doomed to hear the rest of the story. I think the book must have been a million pages long, because it never seemed to end. Every other day, we listened to how the magpie stole things and the aftermath. They stole mirrors, car keys, makeup, screwdrivers, firecrackers, magnifying glasses, and basically anything shiny. I think the worst one was when they stole tin foil. It was so boring I couldn't wait for it to end. Poor Mrs. Reed would just light up and beam like a lighthouse when she reached the end of the chapter. All of us would brighten up and clap, not because we liked it, because we were so happy it was over.

We had all become restless because the end of the school year was coming up and we knew that meant end of school parties. These were the best! The room mothers would all get together and decide on a theme for a day and all the snacks, activities, and art projects revolved around them. I think they tried to coordinate with the teachers to pick something that was "educational". This year's theme was "A day at the Zoo". I thought this was neat because I had never been to a zoo. We didn't have one in our town, and the closest one was all the way in Fort Worth, so I hadn't been. We had watched some films about zoos and the animals that might be in them. We were drawing pictures of lions, tigers, monkeys, elephants, and giraffes that were hung around the room. The room mothers also had us paint some life sized animals on some big pieces of butcher paper that were going to be hung up in the hallways. It was neat.

Most kids know that the last day of school is the best because it marked the first day of freedom to play all summer long. I was looking forward to it, because of vacation, swimming lessons, biking, and roller skating. The last day of school couldn't come fast enough. I was in for two surprises that were going to make my summer start in a bad way. Boy, oh boy!

The last week of school, Mrs. Reed told us that the scores from the state testing had come in and she had an announcement to make about them. We all figured she was going to say something like, "Well, you didn't do well, but you did worse than I expected."

"Students, the scores from the testing came back and you all did very well. However, two particular students excelled in some parts of the test, so I would like to recognize them at this time. Bud, and Tonya, will you come to the front of the class?"

I was stunned. I stood up and walked toward the front. As I passed Janet she gave me thumbs up. Darla fluffed her hair and rolled her eyes. Sean beamed.

"Class, Bud and Tonya scored so well on their state exams that they have been asked to be in a study group at the University in town. Many of you know about Texas Tech, because your parents or family members attended that wonderful university. So this summer for six weeks they will be participating in some testing done by the university to identify students of great intelligence. For the record, Bud scored a perfect score on the math section and Tonya scored a perfect score on the reading and writing sections. I think we should give them a round of applause."

The class clapped wildly, but Bud and I were shocked. I was happy I had scored well, but I was thinking about being some lab rat for six weeks during the summer. Six weeks is an eternity and the exact same as summer school. So, all the preparation for me to stay out of summer school hadn't done me any good. I just couldn't seem to catch a break with a net. Bud looked at me and shrugged. We sat back down and I started thinking about Mama and Daddy. I knew they would be proud, but I didn't want to be studied by strangers. I saw myself in a little cage with a wheel and some hay on the bottom while strangers poked and prodded me and made me run mazes. This didn't seem like a great way to spend summer.

Mrs. Reed seemed very pleased and then told the class to celebrate our success; we could have fifteen minutes of free time in the class to do as we wished, including sitting and talking with our friends. Janet came over and congratulated me and took out her jacks so we could play. We were just setting up when Darla came over and sort of huffed,

"Well, well, a smarty pants playing jacks. I figured you would read that stupid spider book again or maybe the one you wrote all over and tried to give me for Christmas."

She laughed and flounced her way over to her friend who was also laughing. I hung my head. I felt like everything I did, was being thrown up in my face. Janet tried to just change the subject and started playing ones. I felt lower than a roly poly. It was Sean who made me feel better.

"I'm glad I have a smart girlfriend instead of a stupid one," he said pointing at Darla.

I wanted to kiss him. I wanted to so bad that I had to catch myself and hugged him instead. This produced some "OOOOO and AAAHHHHH" from my classmates, but I didn't care. Sean turned beet red and then so did I. Janet grinned behind her hand and Mrs. Reed had to shush us. The day continued until it was time to leave. Mrs. Reed gave me some papers for Mama and Daddy to fill out and sign so I could be in the study group. She smiled widely and congratulated me. It was weird to finally have some respect from Mrs. Reed, who didn't seem to think much of me at the beginning of the school year.

When we got home from school, and while we were having our snack I told Vickie about the study that I was supposed to be in for the summer. She didn't seem impressed.

"It sounds stupid to me. I mean, what are they going to do but give you a bunch of tests to take and then see how you did? It won't mean anything or do anything for you in school, so I wouldn't do it if I were you."

I hadn't thought of it that way, so it seemed that I couldn't exactly fail so what was the big deal?

"I don't know. What if they found out I wasn't that smart and had just gotten lucky on the state tests. Would they tell the school that I was just regular and maybe they would even think I cheated somehow?"

"Well you didn't, did you?"

"No way. Besides, I didn't think it was that hard. Well except the math part that I didn't finish."

"Yeah, but you still did okay on that part, so don't worry about it. Hey, after we're done, want to help me with something?"

"Okay, what is it?"

"I'll show you."

Vickie got up and went to our room. She pulled out a TEEN magazine and opened it to a page she had marked.

"Check this out. There is this article about how to make your room look more grown up and it has this really cool bed that hangs from the ceiling. You put chains on the box spring thing and then you hang it up. It's like having a giant swinging bed."

The picture looked really cool. The chains on the bed were gold and the bed was kind of centered in the room. It looked like it would be so neat.

"Alright, what do you need my help for?"

"So, I was thinking of changing rooms with Rebecca and then hanging the bed in that room, so I need help measuring to see if my bed will fit and how we could hang it up. I want to show Mama and Daddy the whole plan before they think I'm not serious."

I'll admit I wasn't excited about Vickie moving out of our room, because that would mean that Rebecca would be sleeping in our room and would probably be annoying. Also, Vickie was closer to my age and we could talk about stuff in the middle of the night, or watch the thunderstorms out our window. I doubted Rebecca would do that because she was afraid of the thunder. Also, Rebecca was five years younger than me, so we couldn't exactly talk about what was going on at school. Vickie was excited though, so I agreed to help her.

We got Daddy's tape measure out of the garage and measured the bed, the door frame and the place where she wanted to hang the bed. It seemed like it would barely fit, but it was still doable. I didn't realize at the time, that Vickie had some big plans for that room, including putting her own phone in there. When we were done, we started getting things ready for dinner. Mama and Rebecca came home and we started our evening routine.

After dinner, because we didn't have any homework or projects to do, we went outside to play until the street light came on. It came on later now since summer was almost starting. Cheri and I rode our bikes around the block a couple of times. Then the other kids got their bikes and we played bike tag. It was like regular tag, but instead of running you rode your bike. You had to tag the other person which required riding with one hand on the handlebars. This was a trick I had recently picked up and I was working on riding with no hands. Some of the other kids could already do it and they were held in high esteem. Some of us aspired to riding with no hands and no feet, but that was really getting daring. We had all had our share of falling off our bikes with multiple skinned knees and elbows, but thus far no one had been seriously hurt. In fact, no one ever did.

When the street light came on, we all went home. I knew it was time for me to tell Mama and Daddy about the study and so I got out all the papers. I was nervous. I didn't want to do it, but I knew I had to take the papers back to school the next day. I worked up enough courage and finally after the "It's eight o'clock, do you know where your children are" announcement on TV I told Mama and Daddy I had something I needed to tell them.

"Mama, Daddy, I got these papers from Mrs. Reed today. She said it was because I had done well on the state tests that Texas Tech wanted to study me."

"What?" Mama looked surprised and a little alarmed.

I handed Mama the papers and she read some of it.

"Listen to this, John. Tonya scored a 100% on the reading comprehension and writing sections of the test! Isn't that great?!"

"Wowee, you really are a genius!"

I felt my face get red and kind of tingly. I was proud, but also I felt weird. I didn't know what it all meant.

"John, it says here that there are some people in the psychology department at Texas Tech that want to study the top performers of the state tests to see how they have achieved such success. It says that the test subjects would be subjected to a battery of tests to determine the different levels of intelligence in multiple areas. They would test not only reading, and math skills, but spatial intelligence, problem solving, and external influences on intelligence."

"Hmmm," said Daddy thoughtfully. "It sounds like it is going to be pretty serious."

I didn't like the "spatial intelligence" part because it made it sound like they thought I was an alien from outer space and that was why I was so smart. I didn't want to become what had happened to those aliens from Roswell, New Mexico and hidden away never to be seen or heard from again.

Mama continued, "It says that she would need to come to the University every day for an hour for the first six weeks after school let out. They say it would be from 8:00am to 9:00am. Monday through Friday. So that means I could take her on my way to work, and then we would have to figure out how to pick her up. Maybe I can carpool with someone."

I don't know what possessed me to say what I did next, but my big fat mouth did it to me again.

"Hey mama? Bud Jenkins is going to do it too so maybe his Daddy can give me a ride or something."

Now I had really done it. I had just doomed myself to spending an hour riding to and from our experiments with Bud. I had kind of thought it would be nice not to see him much over the summer and maybe he wouldn't be so flirty with me. But there went my big mouth!

"I'll go call Bud's Daddy right now."

Mama seemed really excited. I heard her talking to Bud's Daddy. It seemed like he was excited too. Finally, she hung up.

"It's all settled. I will take you and Bud to the study and Mr. Jenkins will pick you up at 9 and bring you to my office. Then at 11:00 when I get off work, I will bring you and Rebecca home. Vickie, you are old enough to stay at home until we all get home. I will give you some instructions about what to do and what not to do. I will also let Mrs. Campbell know so maybe Michelle can come over to keep you company, or you can go over there. We will work that out later."

Mama started filling out the papers for the study. I was kind of upset, because they hadn't even asked if I wanted to do the study, they just signed me up for it. I think Mama was just excited to see what the psychology department was going to say. I don't know, maybe she thought I was crazy or something.

When she had finished filling out the papers, she put them in the envelope and sealed it shut. She put the envelope on top of my lunch box so I wouldn't forget to take them to school. Then it was time for bed. Vickie and I did our usual routine and got into bed. Mama and Daddy came in for prayers. When they left and we could hear them talking in the living room, Vickie whispered,

"Hey, are you scared about that study thing?"

"Yeah, a little."

"Well, I wouldn't worry. If Mama and Daddy didn't like it, they wouldn't let you do it. Besides, it could be kind of neat. Maybe they will connect you to a bunch of machines and watch your brain waves. Well, anyway, I didn't get to tell them about the hanging bed thing, but maybe I will tomorrow since they are in such good moods."

I knew Vickie was right. Mama and Daddy wouldn't let me do anything that could be dangerous or anything like that. I figured they were just excited and curious too. However, that night I dreamed that the scientists did hook my brain up to a machine, but only after they had removed the top part of my head. It was terrifying.

Magpie Mayhem

It was finally the last day of school. All our desks had been cleared of old papers and assignments and used up glue bottles. We had emptied out our cubby holes of jackets, mittens, and some had even found old lunch box wrappers in them that smelled bad. Mostly, it was a trash clearing out party. Mrs. Reed seemed relieved and in a somewhat happy mood, but we were still under the dictatorship of her timer, so we knew she meant business right up to the end. Everyone was excited to start summer vacation, except me, because of the study. I was nervous about it, but I had the weekend to get some free time in.

At lunch, the cafeteria ladies had prepared what I called their version of "must go". They served lunch buffet style with an assortment of weird food combinations. I suspect they had to clear out the food from this year to make way for next year's supply. I helped myself to enchiladas, peaches, green peas, apple cobbler and a brownie. No one cared that I got two desserts. It was neat. Mrs. Reed agreed that for the last day of school we could abandon our regular boys at one end girls on the other and we could sit with whom we chose. Sean sat next to me, and Janet sat on the other side, so Bud had to sit across from me. In one way, that was the better seat, because whenever I looked up, he was right in my eye line. It was yet another awkward situation for me. I was beginning to get tired of all the drama of having a boyfriend. I was secretly relieved that I was going to have a break during the summer to just relax and not think about boys.

After lunch, it was time for the end of the year party. We had all worked hard on our zoo animal pictures that hung in the hallways. All the room mothers were dressed in safari clothes with khaki pants, and funny little hats they had made from cardboard. They were going to be our guides throughout the zoo we had created. It was neat. At each of the cages, the guide would explain what the animal was what it ate, where it lived and if it was on the endangered list. Then they would either play a tape recording of what the animal sounded like, or they would turn on a projector with some footage taken in other zoos. I recognized some of the footage as coming from "Mutual of Omaha's Wild Kingdom". It was almost like being at a real zoo. I liked it.

Finally, it was about ten minutes before the last dismissal bell. Mrs. Reed called us to the reading circle.

"Class, we have had a good year this year. We have all learned and grown a great deal. I have something special for each of you to take home to remember our time together."

Mrs. Reed pulled out a grocery bag that we could tell was heavy.

"As you know, class, several weeks ago I told you that the book I had been working on had been sent to a publisher for publication. I am happy to announce that they did indeed publish the book and have sent me copies to give to my class as a token of appreciation for their patience. So, I would like to hand you all a copy of the book that I have signed. You now own original hand signed by the author copies of "Magpie Mayhem"!

Mrs. Reed pulled out the book and began passing them out. She was so happy. She beamed at each of us with pride. When I got my copy, I was surprised at how it didn't seem like it had very many pages. After all, we had listened to the book for weeks on end. I opened the book and almost fell off my chair. The publishers had edited her book from a novel to a ten page children's picture book. The only words were "squawk" and "caw" the Magpies made when they were talking to each other. The drawings depicted only one of the dozens of adventures the naughty magpies had gotten into. It was hilarious and pitiful at the same time.

Bud leaned over and whispered,

"They should have paid us cash money for all the time we spent listening to her dumb book."

"Yeah," I agreed, "If they only knew we had listened to it forever, maybe they would."

Mrs. Reed wasn't aware that some of the other kids were stifling giggles when they got their copy. Maybe she did but chose to ignore it.

"Now class, as you can see, the publishers concluded that my story would be best told through pictures rather than words. So I want you to think about this. Sometimes, what you envision is best displayed in ways you never thought. I always saw my story as a young reader chapter book, but after meeting with the publishers, they convinced me that it would sell better as a picture book. I was surprised, but it turns out they were right. The book already has orders from nursery schools across the country."

My mind started to work. Did she mean she was going to get rich off that stupid story that we had been tortured with, only to be drawn in pictures? I looked at Janet, who was rolling her eyes so hard in her head I thought her eyes would stick back there. I couldn't help but giggle. Bud began giggling too for no reason. Soon there were several of us that couldn't take it anymore and were flat out laughing. Poor Mrs. Reed thought we were happy for her.

"Why thank you class for being so supportive of this whole process. You have a wonderful summer!"

The final bell rang, and we all darted for the door. Some of the kids threw their copy of the book on the playground as they left. Others of us chanted, "Schools out, schools out, teacher let the mules out!" As I left, I found Sean. I felt a little sad because we wouldn't see each other all summer.

"See you next year!" I tried to sound cheerful.

"Yeah, you too," Sean's eyes looked a little damp.

The regular crew walked home happy, and free.

Summertime Blues

I had spent the weekend with all my friends riding bicycles, playing baseball, freeze tag, TV tag, and all the other usual games. Sunday, of course, meant church, so I had gone to my regular class with Mr. Al and Mr. Roy. They were getting us ready to be promoted to the next grade level and so they gave us Bible verses to memorize. It was kind of like having homework, but I could usually do it the Saturday night before. They tended to give us pretty easy ones like John 3:16, and Genesis 1:1. I mean if you can't get those, what the heck is wrong with you? It was Sunday night after church that Mama reminded me of my morning doom.

"Tonya, remember tomorrow you are going to Tech to start the intelligence study."

"Oh, yeah, what should I wear?"

Mama thought for a few minutes.

"Well, since you are coming to my office afterwards, you probably need to wear some pants and a shirt, not shorts. I also want you to make sure you brush your hair out really well. I don't want people to think there is a rat's nest on top of your head."

"Okay, Mama," I sort of groaned.

"Now don't you worry. It might be fun."

Mama seemed excited about the fact that I was going to be poked and prodded for the next six weeks.

"Oh, I almost forgot. Bud is going to wait for us at the corner so we can pick him up."

I thought about poor Bud having to wait in front of the Suicide House. Well, maybe he will see a ghost and get scared. I smiled to myself.

The next morning, I got up, got dressed, brushed my hair and went to breakfast. Rebecca was eating her cereal. She still had on her pajamas, so I knew it was my job to get her dressed while Mama finished loading the dishwasher and finishing her makeup. Rebecca was excited to be riding with the big kids to her nursery school.

"Hey, Tonya can I ride between you and Bud?" she asked.

"Sure," I answered thinking I had saved myself.

"No, you have to sit up front with me, because I am taking you first then getting Tonya and Bud where they need to be. I think the people might need some further information so I told my boss Miss Beverly I would be late today."

So I guess I had to share the backseat with Bud. Well it couldn't be any worse than sitting next to him in the truck with Daddy.

We finished breakfast and I got Rebecca ready for preschool. Soon we loaded up in the car and picked up Bud on the corner. He was weirdly chipper. I was less so.

"Hey, Mrs. Agnew!"

"Bud, you should really address older ladies with a 'good morning' rather than 'hey'.

Mama was always trying to make ladies and gentlemen out of all us neighborhood kids.

"Yes, Maam, I mean good morning," Bud seemed a little intimidated.

I was glad Bud was being respectful to Mama, because if he wasn't she was sure to discipline him just as she would us. This was back when parents could discipline any kid without worrying about how the kid's parents would react. It was kind of understood that the adults were in charge of whatever kid was around. For example, once my friend Cheri's mama spanked me along with Cheri because we were playing with Barbie and Ken in a way she didn't like. She told my Mama and I got another spanking from her. It didn't help that Mrs. Campbell showed Mama the naked dolls and demonstrated exactly what they had been doing. Mama was so embarrassed she grabbed me by the arm and dragged me home crying. I knew I was going to get it, and I did.

We dropped Rebecca off at her preschool and Mama drove us to Texas Tech. It was HUGE! I was so nervous walking onto the grounds that I dragged a bit behind. Finally, we made it to the Psychology Department and went upstairs. There was a table in the hallway with an older lady behind it.

"Hello, my name is Dolores Agnew and I have Tonya and Bud Jenkins to drop off for the study."

"Yes, Maam. Can you please fill out this form for each of them? We will call you when we are ready to take them to the testing area."

"Of course. Can you tell me how long that will be? I need to get to work."

"Yes, is should only be a couple of minutes after you fill out the form, then one of our college volunteers will come and get them."

Mama filled out the forms and then we all waited in the hard wooden seats. There were several other kids with their mothers waiting to be called. Bud and I passed the time playing a game of rock, paper, scissors. In just a little bit I heard my named being called. I looked up. It was at that moment that I knew I wanted to go to college. The young volunteer who had called my name looked like a grown up version of Sean. He was tall, had dreamy brown eyes, and when he smiled, he had two deep dimples in his cheeks. I was instantly in love. Mama saw me and kind of smiled.

"Go ahead, Tonya. I will see you after while at the office."

Mama gave me a quick hug and I followed the young man back to the testing area. I felt nervous and shy.

"My name's Matt," he began. "I'm going to be the guy taking you around to the places for the tests you will be taking. The research people will tell you what to do for each test and when you are done, I'll come get you and take you to the next one. The first test is cool. I think you will like it."

I was so smitten by Matt he could've told me that they were going to cut off my legs and I wouldn't have cared. I did catch the part where he would be escorting me around which meant I would get to see him multiple times a day. This was shaping up to be a good day.

Matt took me to a room with just a table and a TV on it. I sat in the chair and when Matt opened the door to go out a young woman came in. She was really pretty and had on lots of eyeliner just like my Uncle Randy's wife.

"Hi! You must be Tonya."

"Yes maam,"

"My name is Rhonda. This is your first test. What I want you to do is to watch the television screen. It is going to play a segment from a popular children's show. When the video ends, I want you to write a description of what you saw."

This was going to be easy, since I was always watching TV and I was pretty good at watching people too.

"Here is a piece of paper so when it ends you can begin writing. Don't worry about correct spelling or anything like that. Just write what you can remember. Okay?"

"Okay," I replied shyly.

Rhonda turned on the TV and a clip from Sesame Street came on. It was the one where a really tall guy was walking down the street looking super cool and reading all the signs. I recognized the guy as EZ Reader. It was a pretty short video, but I had lots to write about. While I watched, Rhonda sat in a chair across from me and took some notes on a clip board. It was weird, but she just smiled when the video was done.

"Okay, now I just want you to write down what you saw."

I began writing. I described EZ Reader, the street he was walking down, the signs he read, and just about anything else I could think of. When I had finished, Rhonda took my paper and attached it to the notes she had taken while I was watching the TV. She went out and Cute Matt came in. We walked across the hall and passed Bud and his guide. Bud gave me thumbs up and went into the room I had just come from. In this room there was a tic tac toe board taped to the floor with duct tape. There was a laundry basket of red bean bags on one side. Cute Matt introduced me to Shannon, the researcher.

"Hi, I'm Shannon. This test is designed to see what your spatial intelligence quotient is."

I looked around for brain wave machines or a surgical table but there was nothing there. I didn't know what to expect.

"Okay, see those bean bags? All I want you to do is to take them one at a time and place them in the center of each square. Then I am going to measure how closely to the center you got each one."

This sounded super easy. I walked to the bean bags and took one out. I carefully placed it in the center square of the tic tac toe board.

"I'm done," I said.

Shannon looked up. She wrote down something on her clip board and got out the measuring tape. She measured all the sides of the bean bag and the center square.

"Okay, you are all done!" she said.

"Was I supposed to use all the bean bags?"

"Well, what do you think?"

I thought for a minute and then said, "Well, you said to put a bean bag in the center of the square, and since there is only one square on the floor, that is what I did."

Shannon wrote down what I said. She smiled and winked. I guessed that meant I had done the right thing.

The morning continued with Cute Matt taking me from test to test. Some of them were fun, like solving mazes, and finding hidden objects in pictures. Others seemed pointless, like describing the color red to a blind man. After a while, Bud's Daddy came and got us, and he took me to my mother's office at the newspaper. Mama introduced me to all the ladies in the office and explained that I had been tested all morning and how smart I was. One of the ladies said,

"Well, since you did so well, here is my jar of candy, and you can have a piece if you like."

Mama nodded, so I took a piece. I was getting hungry for lunch anyway. Mama told me to sit in a chair while she worked for a few more minutes and then she would take me and go pick up Rebecca from the church school and would take us home. I sat and thought about all the tests I had taken, but mostly I thought about Cute Matt. I thought, if that is how Sean is going to look when we grow up, I would be the luckiest girl.

Later, after Mama had picked up Rebecca and we started home, she wanted to know all about the testing I had done. I told her everything, and she was impressed.

"Do you think it will be that way every day for the next six weeks?"

"I don't know, but they did say that tomorrow's tests were all about visual acuriosity."

"Maybe they meant visual acuity?"

"Yeah, that's it. Anyway they said to make sure I got plenty of sleep tonight."

"All right, that sounds interesting. Did you make any new friends while you were there?"

"Not really. We were pretty busy."

"What about that cute boy that came to get you for your first test?"

"Mama!"

I was so embarrassed. It was weird too that Mama thought Cute Matt was cute. I mean, she is married to Daddy after all.

Mama grinned. She was just teasing me. Rebecca piped in.

"Mama, are the people gonna test me too someday?"

"I'm sure of it, since you are so smart too."

Rebecca smiled and nodded her head. She thought she was smart too.

When we got home, Vickie had made lunch for all of us. She had made Vienna sausage sandwiches, with pickles and onions, and she took out some Fritos and poured some tea for us. Mama was surprised, and grateful. The only thing she wanted to go along were the weird banana peppers she liked to eat. When we started eating, Vickie said,

"Hey, that boy Sean that you like called this morning. I told him you were at the testing thing, so he said he would call you later."

I thought it was so sweet that Sean already missed me. He must have wanted to know about the tests, and to make sure Bud had behaved. He was the best boyfriend in the world!

After lunch, I asked Mama if I could call Sean. She said no, that girls don't call boys, and added that he had said he would call later anyway. Mama told me to go take a nap and after that, I could go outside and play. I was kind of relieved, because I felt tired, and I wanted to think about some things. I lie down in my bed and promptly fell fast asleep. A little while later Mama came and woke me up.

"Honey, Sean is on the phone for you. Do you want to talk to him or should I take a message?"

I jumped out of bed and ran to Mama and Daddy's bedroom. Mama winked and closed the door.

"Hey Sean, how's it going?"

"Well its going okay I guess. How was the testing thing today?"

I told Sean all about the different tests and everything except Cute Matt. I told him about going to my Mama's office and getting candy. Finally, I gave Sean a chance.

"That sounds like it was pretty neat. I have something to tell you though. My Daddy took a job in Albuquerque and we will be moving there two weeks from today. I'm sorry I won't be able to see you at school next year."

I was stunned. Albuquerque is in New Mexico and I would probably never see Sean again. Sean asked,

"Are you okay?"

"Umm, no? I mean, it's great that your Dad got a new job, but it means we won't see each other anymore."

"Yeah, I guess this means we can't be boyfriend and girlfriend anymore either."

Sean sounded sad. In a weird way that made me feel good.

"Well Sean, you have been a great first boyfriend. I will never forget you. Even if I never see you again, I won't forget you."

And that last part is true. I never saw Sean again, but I haven't forgotten him after 43 years and counting.

CHAPTER 21

Vacation

Although my heart had been broken at the begin-ning of summer, I managed to make it through the first six weeks. I went to the university every day with Bud and was given tests of various kinds. They tested my vision, hearing, sense of touch, and taste, they tested how I wrote about multitudes of things like describing things or writing about a typical day in school. By the end, I was relieved that it was the last day. But alas, it was also the last day I would see Cute Matt. Cute Matt had been so nice the whole six weeks. He told me at one point that the reason he was working in the Psychology department was that he wanted to help kids who were smart, but were from poor families. I thought that was the nicest thing ever. On the last day, Cute Matt and all the other testers threw us a little party with cupcakes and ice cream. It was fun. However, it wasn't as fun as what was coming up. Vacation!

Vacation meant two things: spending a whole week with my friend Cheri in Colorado, and horseback riding! This year, we were going to a new place that Cheri's Daddy had heard about. It was called Fun Valley. It was just outside of South Fork, Colorado up in the mountains. There were places to camp, fish, hike, play miniature golf, an arcade, a playground, and of course horses! It sounded amazing and I was looking forward to going. However, there was the long drive up to Colorado, so we had to leave really early. Daddy and Cheri's Daddy wanted to leave at six in the morning.

We had packed our camper, fixed the back of the truck for me and Vickie and Rebecca to sit and sleep in on the road, and even gathered some firewood so we would have it ready when we got to the campsite. There were three folding lawn chairs and a small crate in the back of the truck for us to play cards, and Daddy had put a piece of plywood in the back with a mattress on top for us to sleep on. The windows on the new camper shell opened so we would have ventilation, and the sliding ones on the back helped too. The only problem was that the window between the truck and the camper shell didn't connect right, so we couldn't talk to Mama and Daddy as we rode. That was okay though, because we had a stick of wood that we used to bang on the truck if we needed anything, or if there was an emergency. Mama was worried about us, but Daddy gave us strict instructions about what to do and what not to do. I figured we had it better than Cheri's family because they were all crammed into the back seats of their long station wagon. I was excited.

Finally, it was time. We got into the truck and Daddy closed and locked the tailgate and the camper shell door. Rebecca climbed up on the mattress to sleep some more and so did Vickie. I was too excited to sleep, so I just watched out the side windows. For a long time, we just drove and not much happened. As the day got hotter, I opened the side windows to let in the air. It was nice. I had kept myself busy watching for rabbits and antelope in the fields outside, and playing an occasional game of solitaire with the cards I had brought. It was during one of those games I made a frightening discovery. The firewood we had loaded in the back with us kids had black jumping spiders with green eyes in it. I noticed the first one when I dropped a card and bent to pick it up. A spider about the size of a dime jumped on my hand and scared the beejesus out of me. I stood up and bumped my head on the top of the camper shell. Vickie and Rebecca didn't wake up though, so I suffered in silence and rubbed my head. I wasn't afraid of the spiders, I just didn't like the way they jumped. Also, if I made any sudden moves, they would turn and glare at me with those green eyes.

Finally, after half and eternity, Rebecca woke up.

"I need to go to the bathroom," she said.

"Okay, I'll let Mama and Daddy know."

I banged the wood on the bottom of the truck which made Mama and Daddy both jump. Rebecca laughed. So did I. However, it was harder for them to understand what we needed until Rebecca did the "pee pee dance". You know the universal holding of the privates and wiggling your knees back and forth? Daddy pulled the truck over.

We were on a long stretch of road with only fields and occasional cows along the side. There weren't any bushes to speak of in that particular part of Texas. So Mama kind of held up a towel around Rebecca so no one would see her behind. We would have stopped at a gas station had there been one nearby. I figured I had better go too and Mama woke Vickie up to go as well. Cheri's family had stopped behind us, and they were all going too. It was a regular pee pee festival; four of us and six of them all peeing all over the side of the road. Mama made sure we were in the camper before the boys were allowed to go. I had no desire to watch anyone pee so I just sat in one of the chairs. Mama decided that she would ride in the back with Rebecca and me for a while, so Vickie got up front. I was glad because I could get some sleep while Mama played with Rebecca. I forgot to tell them about the spiders.

We had been back on the road about ten minutes when Mama banged on the floor of the truck furiously. Daddy swerved over quickly because of the intensity. Mama had spotted the spiders.

"John! John! There are black widows in the wood back here!"

They weren't black widows, but to Mama any black spider was a killer. Daddy chuckled and explained to Cheri's family why we had stopped. Everyone laughed except Mama. Daddy took out the wood and kind of shook it out and then restacked it. Mama was still reeling, but agreed to get back in and continue.

We drove for about six hours and it was time to stop for lunch. Mama and Daddy had heard about a place where the corners of Colorado, New Mexico, Texas and Kansas met and there was a giant truck stop there with a café. We pulled into a bustling parking lot just beyond where the truckers stopped and made our way to the café. Before we went in, me, Cheri, Vickie, Michelle, and Rebecca all went to the restroom that was just across the parking lot. As we were waiting, a large group of women entered. They were loud, and excited and very animated. One of the largest women I had ever seen asked if she could cut in front of us as she had an "emergency". We let her in front of us and when the stall opened, she went in. Much to my amazement, the loudest, longest fart I had ever heard came from the stall.

"Oh Lordy! I have been holding that in! I couldn't let loose on the bus!"

The rest of the ladies started laughing and squealing, so I didn't feel so bad when I giggled. Vickie and Michelle kind of pinched me and so I stopped. Vickie leaned down and whispered,

"Stop it! You don't want to embarrass her!"

Michelle looked at Vickie and nodded her head. The lady came out of the stall.

"Now listen, child, don't go in that stall. I have fouled it something terrible."

This was too much. After we all left the restroom, we joined Mama and Cheri's family in the café. I wanted to tell everyone what happened, but Vickie said not to. I decided to wait until later to tell Mama when we were riding in the truck. I hadn't counted on Rebecca to say anything.

We went through the cafeteria line and picked some food that didn't look too bad. It wasn't easy as truckers will eat anything, so most of the food was either fried, or mashed. Even the green beans were mashed. The potatoes with gravy looked passable, but not encouraging. However, we were all tired and hungry, so we just muddled through. When we sat down at the long table, Daddy lead a blessing and we began to eat. I went for the mashed potatoes and gravy first.

"Mama, these are terrible!" I bellowed.

Mama was furious. I tried to explain that the potatoes were stone cold and the gravy was lukewarm at best, but she wasn't having it.

"Quiet! The ladies in the cafeteria may hear you. It would hurt their feelings."

"Mama?" Rebecca piped in, "That fat lady over there farted really loud in the bathroom!"

Rebecca had saved my life. Daddy started laughing and pretty soon the whole table was laughing. Mama turned red and giggled too. We finished lunch and got back on the road. We had about six hours left before reaching our destination so we kind of rushed. We got to the truck just in time to see the fat lady boarding her church bus. As we pulled away we could hear them singing "When the Roll is Called up Yonder." I don't know why I thought that was funny, but I did.

Mama and Rebecca joined Daddy up front, so me and Vickie had the back to ourselves. We started playing War with our cards, and we were barely even aware of how much time was passing. We sang "Desperado" and "Delta Dawn" and just about every other song we could think of. We remembered some old songs we had learned at Camp Monakiwa a few summers ago too. Our favorite was "Murphy's Saloon". We had to sing it when Mama wasn't around because it went like this,

> *Over hill over dale we will fight for ginger ale,*
> *In the cellar of Murphy's saloon.*
> *We are brave, we are bold, for the liquor we can hold,*
> *In the cellar of Murphy's saloon.*
> *So it's drink, drink, drink, til we vomit in the sink (Bleh),*
> *Shout out your orders loud and clear!*
> *We'll be rolling on the floor when the cops bust through*
>   *the door*
> *In the cellar of Murphy's Saloon (More Beer!)*
> *In the cellar of Murphy's saloon! (Hey!)*

Needless to say, Mama didn't approve of young ladies singing a song about drinking. We loved it though, because it made us feel like we were bad.

Finally, it was getting late and we stopped for the night. We stopped in the town of South Fork, and there was a small motel there that was cheap enough for us to spend one night. It also had several restaurants on a crossroad so we were set. Daddy checked us into the motel and we went into our room. Mama and Daddy were tired, but Daddy said there was one thing to do before we got settled. Much to our surprise, Daddy jumped up on one of the beds and began jumping up and down acting like a monkey.

"John! What the heck are you doing?"

Daddy just laughed and pointed to the other bed and said, "Girls, go try it out."

We jumped on the beds for a few minutes and when we stopped, we were all laughing. Mama just looked at us with "the look", but Daddy said,

"Hey, we are on vacation. We get to do what we want."

We had dinner with Cheri's family at a little diner then got ready for bed. We were exhausted, so we all went to sleep right away.

The next morning, we got up and dressed and met Cheri's family at a restaurant called "The Hungry Logger". They served pancakes the size of a large dinner plate with fruit compote on the top with whipped cream. I ate until I was about to bust. Mama helped me with my pancakes and so did Daddy. When we were done we loaded up and headed out. Today, we only had about an hour drive and then we would set up camp.

Fun Valley

When our campers pulled into the entrance of Fun Valley, I knew I had found heaven. Off to the left of the road was a huge barn and I could see six or seven horses saddled and just about to head out for a trail ride. To the right was the registration office and gift shop. Just a couple of doors down were a dance hall, and a place to rent fishing gear to fish in the stock pond out behind. There was a little grill that sold barbeque sandwiches and just beyond that a really cool looking miniature golf course. Daddy and Cheri's Daddy went to get us signed in and Cheri and I went to the gift shop. It was full of little knick knacks, and toy bows and arrows, Indian headdresses, Indian dolls, drums, and weird gag gifts. We looked around a bit and then it was time to go set up camp.

We drove down a long road into the camping area. Daddy and Cheri's Daddy had gotten two campsites next to each other. They both helped each other park and level the campers. This usually took around an hour. Meanwhile, Mama told me and Cheri we could go check out around the place, but not to go near the river without a parent. Cheri and I headed out first to the big building at the entrance to the camping area.

It was a two story building with the showers and bathrooms on the bottom level, and a long staircase that led to an upper room. Cheri and I wanted to see what was there, so up we went. To our amazement and delight, there was an arcade. It had a cool bowling game, a foosball table, a pool table, but most impressive of all a video game called "Pong". We couldn't believe it! We had heard about this new kind of game, but had never seen one. There was a boy playing and he had a stack of quarters waiting in reserve. We watched him play in amazement as the electronic ball bounced back and forth while he moved a stick up and down to hit the ball back. We were mesmerized. We couldn't even conceive how it worked. I knew I had to play. Cheri did too.

After we watched for a while, we went exploring further. We walked down to a bridge that overlooked the river. Then we walked the loop around the camping area and took note of all the other kids. There were several small ponds that were stocked with rainbow trout and we saw fishermen at each one. Finally, we decided to walk to the barn where the horses were. I wanted to find out how much it cost to ride. I was hoping Mama and Daddy would let us go. As we went along, we saw several other families with kids so we knew we could make some temporary friends if we wanted to. Cheri and I held hands and walked along as happy as clams. When we got to the barn, one of the girls that worked there struck up a conversation with us. Her name was Carrie.

"Hey y'all! Are you interested in a ride?"

"We sure are! How much does it cost?"

"Well, we have two rides. The first is 30 minutes long and costs ten dollars, and the second is and hour long that costs twenty dollars. Most people take the shorter ride. We go along the river and up the mountain for a ways before heading back down. Are y'all good riders?"

I had ridden a few times at my cousin's ranch, but I don't think Cheri had ever ridden.

"Well, I've ridden some but my friend Cheri hasn't."

"That's okay. We have some really gentle horses that are good for inexperienced riders."

Carrie showed us around the barn a little, but the horses were out on a ride so we didn't get to see any of them. She did show us the place where there were about six goats living. She gave us some hay and let us feed the goats. There was one brown and white one named Bart. He was remarkable mostly because he farted a lot. We nicknamed him Farting Bart. It seemed that the word fart had become our word of the year. It was as close to cursing as we could come without getting in trouble.

Soon it was time to go check in with Mama. We walked back toward the campsite but we stopped to play on the giant see saws that were just off the road. We had so much fun. When we got back to camp, Mama was making sandwiches for lunch. Vickie and Rebecca were already there. Vickie and Michelle had gone exploring too and she had some things to report. She had gone down to the river to watch the fishermen and to look for boys. She said there were some cute ones.

"I hope you are talking about cute fish," teased Mama.

"Right on, Mama." Vickie had picked up some interesting slang from listening to the radio.

"Now, you girls listen. Don't go down to that river without a grown up. I don't want y'all to fall in and drown on vacation. That goes double for you Tonya and Rebecca."

"Okay Mama," I replied kind of half- hearted.

"I mean it. The river is really high right now and you could get swept away in no time. It would be terrible if something were to happen."

Mama was right. After lunch, she and Cheri's Mama took us all down to the river to watch Daddy fish. The river was very high and the water was rushing along with tremendous speed. If you fell in, you were toast. We watched the fishermen and Daddy caught two while we were there. He was hoping to catch enough for tonight's dinner. Mama had counted on having fish for three nights during the week, so she wouldn't have to buy any food from the general store in South Fork. Free food was our best savings on vacation.

Cheri and I spent the rest of the afternoon, playing Frisbee, chase and hide and seek. The mountain air was hard on us because of the altitude, so we were soon very tired. Around four thirty, our Daddy's came in from fishing and Daddy was happy to announce that he had caught six fish which meant we were having it for dinner. I asked Daddy if I could help him clean them.

"That's grody gross!" Vickie said, "I'm not doing that!"

Despite being pretty tough, Vickie had a kind of weak stomach. In fact, if she got to bothering me too much, I would make pretend throw up sounds and she would stop. Sometimes she would wretch a little which was awesome.

"I just want to see what the fish are eating so I know which bait to use in the morning."

Daddy and I went back down to the river with the fish and his fish knife. He showed me how to first take the scales off the fish. Next he cut the fish open and grabbed hold of the gills and pulled the guts out with one pull. We looked at the stomach contents. Which was mostly bugs, but a few of the fireball fish eggs we used were there too. I was glad because I didn't like putting grasshoppers on a hook. They always grabbed your finger in a desperate last chance of survival. I felt sorry for them. So I knew I could catch some fish with eggs. It seemed weird to me that fish ate their own eggs.

At any rate, we cleaned all six and then took them to Mama to cook. Mama coated them in cornmeal and fried them on the campfire with our heavy cast iron skillet. She made hush puppies and we had some coleslaw too. It was the best fish I ever ate. After supper, the sun went down and it got cold so we put on our jackets and listened to Cheri's older brother sing with his guitar. He had an amazing voice. He was really talented. Some older girls from nearby campsites came up to listen. They were looking goo goo eyed at him and Cheri's brother Michael. I guess I looked a little jealous, because Michael looked at me and winked as if to say not to worry. At least that's what I dreamed.

The next morning, I woke up early as I heard Daddy go outside to build the morning fire for coffee. I got dressed as quickly and quietly as possible and gently closed the door to the camper. Mama, Vickie and Rebecca were still asleep. Daddy held up his finger to his lips to shush me. He motioned for me to get the fishing gear. I got my and his pole, the tackle box and we were set to go. Daddy made me some hot cocoa and him some coffee before putting the fire out. We walked away from the campsite before either of us spoke.

"You ready to catch some trout this morning?"

"Yep," was all I had to offer so early. I think it was around six in the morning.

The sun was just barely peeking over the mountain and it was really chilly. We walked down to the river and luckily no one else was fishing yet, so we could pick our spot. Daddy motioned to a spot where the river created an eddy. There were already fish jumping to catch their breakfast, so we both casted our lines in that direction.

The thing that is different about river fishing is that the current pulls your line along and so you have to pay attention not to get hung up in the rocks. After a few minutes, I felt the unmistakable pull of a fish on my line. I reeled and set the hook. Daddy came over to help if I needed it. I played the fish just as Daddy had taught me, and landed my first fish of the day. Daddy measured it to make sure it was the right size to keep. It measured 7.5 inches which was a good fish. We strung him on the stringer then anchored it to the shore so he was still in the water, but couldn't get away. Soon, Daddy had caught a couple of fish. We decided that we would clean the fish and have them for breakfast.

We cleaned the fish and when we got to camp everyone was awake and was jealous that we had already gotten our fish. Daddy just grinned and fried the fish. My fish had beautiful pink flesh which was delicious. I felt really proud of the fact that I was eating fish and everyone else had boring scrambled eggs and bacon. I tell you, the smell of fresh caught fried fish in the morning is something only those of us, who have had it, fully understand. It is one of life's pleasures that have to be experienced rather than explained. The rest of the day was spent much as the day before, fishing, hiking, playing Frisbee, walking up and down the road to see the horses and goats, just general playing, and eventually supper and a campfire. We played card games like go fish, war, killer, and even some dominoes. Vacation was heaven.

CHAPTER 23

School Days

Summer had come and gone and now it was time to get ready for a new school year. I was headed into fourth grade while Vickie was going into Junior High. She was very excited and a little nervous about it. Rebecca had one more year at the preschool before starting kindergarten. The day came for students and parents to meet the new teacher for the year. I was relieved that I would be moving to a new wing of the school and wouldn't have to see Mrs. Reed too often. The fourth through sixth grade hall was separated by an outdoor courtyard. I wouldn't have to see Mrs. Reed at all most days. I was happy about that.

The meet the teacher night was always busy, yet exciting. It was like staring with a clean slate. I knew the name of my new teacher, but I didn't know anything about her because she was a new teacher. We were going to be her first class. This was kind of cool. I was anxious to meet her. Mama and Daddy went with me that night. We came to the classroom which was arranged differently than the straight rows of Mrs. Reed's class. The desks were called airplane desks that had a seating place separated by two cubby holes between, with one large table top. Our teacher had arranged so that there were two airplane desks facing each other creating groups of four students. My name was at the front next to a boy named David. Across from me was Patty, and next to her was a boy named Joe. When our teacher came in, I was surprised. She was very tall and young and pretty. Her name was Ms. Gaither.

Ms. Gaither explained that her class was going to be a series of learning centers that the students would rotate through during the course of the day. She explained that this would foster self- learning which research had shown was more effective than teacher lead learning. Ms. Gaither sounded really smart. She went through the various centers which were reading, writing, science, social studies, and games. I couldn't believe it. We were going to play games in school?

"I want the students to learn that learning can be fun and not just drilling and preparing for testing. Of course, we will certainly not neglect the state testing preparations, but it will be infused within the centers."

Ms. Gaither was amazing. I couldn't imagine not being tied to a timer all year. Some of the parents weren't convinced.

"How do you know this way of teaching is better if you've never taught before?"

Ms. Gaither was unfazed.

"When I completed my student teaching experience last year, we took the data from my students and compared it to teachers whose classes were taught more traditionally. My students scored higher in every section of the test. We determined that adding the element of self- discovery was a key to their success."

This seemed to placate the parent and the rest of the time was spent exploring the classroom and the centers. I thought it was neat. I also got to see some of my classmates from last year. Some of them I was glad to see, some, like Stupid Darla, I wasn't. The boy next to me had just moved from Amarillo, so he didn't know anyone. I introduced him to some of the boys I did know. Soon it was time to go home.

"Well, what do you think, Tonya," Mama asked.

"I think it is going to be a great year!"

"I think so too. You know your Uncle Gerald knows Ms. Gaither and he says she is going to be a great teacher."

This was high praise, because my Uncle Gerald had been Teacher of the Year. The fact that he said Ms. Gaither was good made me feel excited about the new school year.

The next night, Mama and Daddy went with Vickie to meet all her new teachers. You see, in Junior High, you got six teachers, one per subject. Vickie was excited to tour the Junior High and see her new teachers. Mama had asked me to stay at home with Rebecca and if I needed to I could go next door to Mrs. Boyter's house if I got scared. Mama had given me instructions to keep the front door closed and locked, watch TV with Rebecca, then get her dressed for bed. Mama said she would put her to bed when they got home. I felt very important. I was in charge of Rebecca for a whole hour at night by myself. I was also a little scared. I didn't want to have to go to Mrs. Boyter's house because she smoked a lot and had a raspy voice that made me feel weird.

After dinner, Mama, Daddy and Vickie left. The house seemed really quiet with just me and Rebecca there. I was glad to have Tiffany, our poodle, there to alert us in case we needed it. Rebecca and I sat down to watch TV, but we could only find shows that was either boring, or that Mama wouldn't let us watch. There was a show I thought would be neat called, Laugh In, but after watching a few minutes, I just didn't get the jokes, and they mostly talked about the government. I did like the pretty go-go dancer named Goldie, though. She had beautiful eyes, and always seemed to be smiling. She also danced really well too. I could tell though that Mama probably wouldn't have liked it that we were watching, so I suggested we play a game.

Rebecca was game. We decided to play hide and seek with Tiffany. We loved that game. One of us would hold Tiffany and the other would hide. Then when we were ready, the hider would call to Tiffany to come find us. Tiffany seemed to like this game too. Rebecca wanted to hide first.

"Okay, just remember that you can't go outside."

Rebecca went to hide in the front closet where Mama kept her sewing machine. She called out.

"Tiffany! Come find me!"

Tiff took off like a shot, running with her nose full on the ground. She found Rebecca in no time flat. Then it was my turn. I decided to hide in Mama and Daddy's shower since it was the furthest away from the living room. I called out to Tiffany.

"Come on, Tiff!"

I could hear her running through the house with Rebecca hot on her heels. A couple of times Tiff would check in the bathroom, but not find me. Finally she did, and got lots of pats and scratches behind the ear. After a few more turns it was time to dress Rebecca for bed. Mama had said not to worry about baths since she didn't want anyone to drown while she was gone. Rebecca got her Strawberry Shortcake pajamas on and I got a book out to read to her. It was just about that time Mama, Daddy and Vickie got home.

"Tonya, Rebecca, we're home!" Mama called.

"Hey Mama, I just got Rebecca ready for bed."

"Good. Come on Rebecca let's go read a story and then its bedtime."

Mama finished putting Rebecca to bed with a story and prayers while me and Vickie got ready for bed too. Daddy turned on the TV for the "It's 8 o'clock, do you know where your children are" announcement.

"Yep, they're right here!" Daddy always felt the need to answer the TV.

Vickie went into her room with her cool hanging bed. I stopped at the door to see if she wanted to talk. She had made it clear (with a couple of frogs to the leg), that I had to have permission to enter her room now.

"Alright, you can come in," she said.

"Well, how was it?"

"It was cool, Madool, man! I met all my teachers and they were pretty nice, but the best was the tennis coach. He is going to be my Social Studies teacher too. He has this cool perm in his hair and a mustache. He said he was going to have tennis tryouts early in the year so we can practice all year before tournaments. That means we will beat everyone for sure."

"Wow, maybe you'll win trophies just like Mama!"

"I hope so. The school has three different hallways and a huge gym. The cafeteria was huge too. And you know that rumor about the Monkey Cage? It's true. There is a fenced off part in front and some of the older kids warned the younger ones not to stand too close or we would be put in."

I wasn't sure Vickie was telling the truth because all the parents were there too. Vickie also had that sideways look she got when she was telling a half truth. Both of us were excited about the new school year. We would still walk together; Vickie just had to walk a block further to the Junior High. It was shaping up to be a good year.

CHAPTER 24

A New Year, a New Love

*I*t was mid-September and the regular routine of school had started and was moving like clock-work. All us kids in the neighborhood met at the corner to walk to school together as usual. However, this year, Bud joined us. I didn't mind as much as I thought I would. We had actually forged a somewhat awkward friendship. Bud still liked me, but he knew he couldn't be my boyfriend. I was still stinging from the loss of Sean.

However, the new kid David was kind of cute and lots of people said we would make a cute couple since we were the shortest kids in the class. David was nice, but he didn't have dreamy brown eyes. He did have really nice auburn red hair though. He kind of fashioned it like David Soul from Starsky and Hutch. However, I had my eye on a boy named Joe. He had black hair and dark eyes, and he always wore a really cool black belt with his jeans and white shirt. He was kind of shy, but seemed really smart. His best friend was the funniest kid in school, Frankie.

Frankie was hilarious. He always had a funny joke or was doing something to make the class laugh. The best thing though was he could make Ms. Gaither laugh too. She had a great sense of humor, so our class seemed relaxed and fun. Once, in the science learning center, we were supposed to build a structure as high as we could with marshmallows and pretzel sticks. Somehow, Frankie managed to make his touch the ceiling of the classroom.

"Hey, look Ms. Gaither! I'm King Kong!" shouted Frankie as he crashed and ate the marshmallows from his enormous building.

"Oh Frankie," was all Ms. Gaither could get out between giggles.

These kind of things happened on a regular basis. Our class was a bustling center of activity. Our principal Dr. Overby often stopped by to check out the goings on. He seemed impressed. I was glad to get to go to the reading center and read whatever I wanted without worrying about getting into trouble.

"Well, look who finally got a new book," Stupid Darla commented.

I was reading a book by Beverly Cleary, my favorite author. I connected with Ramona in the books because she was no nonsense and had a funny way of looking at the world like me.

"Have you read any of these?" I asked Stupid Darla.

"No, I only read grown up books that my sister has, not baby books."

"Darla," said Ms. Gaither, "Perhaps reading books more appropriate for your age would benefit you more."

Anyone who called out Stupid Darla was okay with me. I loved Ms. Gaither.

"Hey Darla, maybe those kissy kissy books aren't good for you," chimed Frankie.

Darla looked lower than a ladybug's stomach. I loved it. She didn't even realize Frankie had a huge crush on her. She was too stupid. Hah!

One of the best things about Ms. Gaither's class was we could sit with whomever we wished at lunch. No restrictions at all. Ms. Gaither had explained that eating was to be enjoyable with good company, so we SHOULD sit with our friends. Some of the other teachers thought this was promoting boy-girl relationships. I think it just meant we could enjoy part of school. Me, Patty, Janet, Beverly, Randy, and John always sat together. Occasionally, Patty would sit with other groups, but mostly with us. Frankie, Joe, George, and David sat with us sometimes. We had fun, although sometimes the cafeteria ladies would get on to us for being too loud. Once we got into trouble because we had created a dessert of brownies with mustard dots on top. One of the ladies saw us and made us all eat our creations so as to not waste food. Yuck.

I was having a great year in Ms. Gaither's class and didn't grumble or complain about school anymore. Mama told me that if I got straight "A's" I could start piano lessons. I wanted to learn so badly. Mama said she was saving up to rent a piano so I had to do my part. I was working hard in school and was having such a good year I was sure to get all A's.

Vickie was having a good year too. She had tried out for the tennis team and made it. She was glad to see Coach Cox every afternoon after school for practice.

Acknowledgements

I would like to thank my loving and supportive husband, Roger, who has had to listen to the stories related in this book numerous times. His patience, understanding, and encouragement have been consistent if not relentless.

Additionally, I would like to thank my girls, Jessica and Heather, as they have heard these stories as well, and have offered advice whether asked for or not. Their opinions are lovingly valued or ignored as the situation dictates.

The countless people who have influenced me over the years cannot be ignored. I would especially like to thank Ms. Linda Gaither, my fourth-grade teacher, for being creative and kind. The late Gerald Judd, my Uncle, should also be acknowledged because of his love of teaching, love of books and the influence he had on a budding writer.

Most importantly, Mama, Daddy, Vickie, and Rebecca deserve the most thanks for giving me the most magical childhood. I love you all very much and am forever grateful for your love, support and friendship. Love always wins.